DANIEL DAVIES was born in Sutton Coldfield, near Birmingham, in 1973, to a Welsh father and a Polish-German mother. He studied English at Cambridge. His previous jobs include curator at the British Museum and sub-editor at medical journal *The Lancet* and the *Evening Standard*. He lived abroad for three years, teaching English in Barcelona, Prague and San Sebastián.

the isle of dogs

daniel davies

A complete catalogue record for this book can be obtained from the British Library on request

First published in 2008 by Serpent's Tail,
an imprint of Profile Books Ltd
3A Exmouth House
Pine Street
London EC1R 0JH
website: www.serpentstail.com

ISBN 978 1 85242 998 0

Designed and typeset by Sue Lamble
Printed by Clays, Bungay, Suffolk

10 9 8 7 6 5 4 3 2 1

The paper this book is printed on is certified by the © 1996 Forest Stewardship Council A.C. (FSC). It is ancient-forest friendly. The printer holds FSC chain of custody SGS-COC-2061

For my parents, who are nothing like
Henry and Rosemary Shepherd

acknowledgments

Pete Ayrton, Tim Bates, Becky Carter, Peter Davies, Susan Davies, Joan Deitch, Andrew Franklin, Rebecca Gray, Katharine Marsh, Niamh Murray, Paul Stewart, Donna Tipping, John Williams.

prologue

IT BEGAN WITH A WEEKEND stay at my parents' house in the English countryside. On Saturday night, I went for a meal in a local Indian restaurant with a female friend who was also visiting her parents. Just after midnight, on our way back to her parked car, we were attacked in the street by three teenagers, one of whom was a girl.

The attack was short, unprovoked and extraordinarily violent. My friend, mercifully, came off the better, though she did suffer a cracked rib and extensive bruising. I, on the other hand, didn't get off quite so lightly. To this day, for reasons that have remained a mystery, I believe I was their real target.

As well as having a Beck's bottle cracked into my skull, causing severe concussion and a gash in my crown that required twelve stitches, I suffered a fractured jaw, chipped front teeth (caused by landing on the pavement, face first) and two broken fingers (caused by the girl repeatedly stamping on my hand in stilettos). They didn't even take our money, so it wasn't a mugging. I sometimes wish they had – at least that would have given the attack some meaning.

I was admitted to a local hospital for treatment and kept there under observation. It was while I was lying in bed that I got talking to the man in the bed opposite. I remember almost nothing about his appearance: the ward was badly lit and I was groggy from the morphine. But I do remember his words. What he divulged, during the early hours of a single night, was that he had once been a high-flying media professional, but had given up that existence to lead what he called an 'alternative lifestyle'. Only later did I discover just how alternative that lifestyle was.

But he didn't simply tell me his life story from start to finish; on the contrary, he was oblique, guarded and laconic. When I asked him whether he'd considered writing down any of his experiences, he told me that he already had, but only when he felt like it. He hadn't collated his writings, nor put them into any kind of order. Given that I worked as an editor in book publishing, I told him, I might be able to help.

Two weeks later, after we'd both been discharged, a brown jiffy bag arrived on my desk in London. Inside was a motley range of materials: notebooks, a diary, printed-out e-mails, a business-style contact card and a CD with Word files on it. There was also a postcard with a picture of his (and my parents') home town on the front. On the back he'd written a single sentence: *I doubt it's worth the effort.*

But I believe it was. The book you're about to read is composed of all these materials. Although I've arranged the text into a narrative order – some of it was dated, some of it wasn't – it remains, at times, elliptical and impressionistic, which is entirely in keeping with the manner of its composition. I've also made extensive editorial changes, but these have primarily been of punctuation and syntax. In places, I've deleted the names of locations and people to preserve their anonymity. Some of the names have been changed altogether.

When the editing process was finished, I sent the typescript to the author. After a week of silence, I received a brief e-mail from him: *Fine. I'll send you a title and two epigraphs. And then it's over.* He did so the following day, after which, of his own volition, he had nothing further to do with *The Isle of Dogs.*

No doubt the dispensation of justice in those days, as also in later times, was largely concerned with regulating the libidinous instinct, and presumably not a few of the prisoners slowly perishing beneath the leaden roof of the palace will have been of that irrepressible species whose desires drive them on, time after time, to the very same point.

W. G. SEBALD, *VERTIGO* (1990)

To what purpose is all the toil and bustle of this world? What is the end of avarice and ambition, of the pursuit of wealth, of power and pre-eminence? Is it to supply the necessities of nature? The wages of the meanest labourer can supply them. What then are the advantages of that great purpose of human life which we call *bettering our condition?*

ADAM SMITH, *THE THEORY OF MORAL SENTIMENTS* (1759)

part one

a complete revision of quantum mechanics

1

I HAVEN'T INTRODUCED MYSELF. My name is Jeremy Shepherd; I'm thirty-nine years old and I live with my parents.

Our house is in deep suburbia, in a provincial town you've probably never heard of. It's about two hours from London by train. But then, most English towns these days are about two hours from London by train. I suppose that makes it pretty much anywhere. Or pretty much nowhere. I doubt you'd have any reason to come here. At best, you might have passed through it on your way to somewhere else.

The town grew threefold during the 1960s – which is to say, it grew exponentially uglier. Architects of that decade should be shot in public; I'll happily pull the trigger. The town is full of treeless estates, concrete precincts, graffitied flyovers. In short, it's full of sharp edges. Many of the windows are smashed, boarded up. If the town could smile, you'd see its rotten teeth. Although it lies in an industrial region of England, it was never bombed during the war. I suspect the Luftwaffe droned over it and simply thought – *Nah!*

My parents' house is in the smarter end of town. They bought it fifteen years ago, when houses were affordable. It has hanging baskets, floral curtains and a doorbell that plays the first four notes of Beethoven's Fifth.

My bedroom has a washbasin and a walk-in wardrobe.

Beside the washbasin is a bowl of potpourri; above my bed is a Kandinsky print. It's nothing flash, but it's adequate: self-contained. I don't long for my own property, my own *space*. How much space does a single human being really need? Less, I suspect, than estate agents tell us. Besides, since I'm an only child, the brutal truth is that, one day, this house will belong to me.

My living arrangement works well. My relationship with my parents is affable, respectful, with a healthy mutual distance. We exchange amusing anecdotes over dinner, our cutlery clinking our plates. In many ways, I'm more like a lodger than a son, although they're unfailingly affectionate towards me. I pay a nominal rent each month, which covers all the bills (the house has no mortgage). I also help with domestic chores, such as the cleaning and shopping. If something doesn't work, it's me who fixes it or calls in the repairman.

When I'm not at home, being a son and handyman, I'm at work. I work locally, at an office on the outskirts of town. The building resembles a concrete bomb shelter – or a disused abattoir. I cycle there every day in bicycle clips, safety helmet and a fluorescent yellow waistcoat.

As for the job itself, the details need detain us little. I am a low-level civil servant, helping to process demographic information about England. The work is administrative, with heavy use of computers. It's tedious and repetitive, but I don't mind this. I prefer my work to be undemanding: it gives me mental time and space to think about other things. In my previous job, I never had time to think, even for a moment. *Farewell the tranquil mind!* bemoans Othello. In my current job, I've greeted it. This is what people forget about boredom: it's a form of stillness, a form of peace.

Because I have a university degree, which still has some clout in this backwater, my superiors have tried repeatedly to promote me. But each time I refused, much to their bewilderment. They kept telling me I would receive more money, to which my answer was always the same: what do I need more money for? (Steaming tea; exchanged looks; silence.) So I have stayed resolutely where I am, in what remains a junior position.

And now, people leave me alone. For all its flaws – its dullness, its inertia, the small-toothed pedantry of its office politics – the English civil service has one, vital, redeeming feature: its inclusiveness. It's the professional equivalent of the Church: everyone is welcome. Whether you're the most ruthless conformist, or the most grotesque misfit, you can always pursue a career in the civil service.

It was also one of the few employers to offer legal jobs to the small number of ethnic-minority inhabitants in my town. In fact, I work with one, a refugee – Tariq, a handsome, black-eyed, Basra-born Iraqi, who was a qualified architect in his own country. He now spends his days nursing jammed printers and crashed computers. But it is better than his first job in England: illegally picking carrots, for two pounds an hour, for the very chain of supermarket whose car park I've come to know so well.

My life, I should say, wasn't always like this. It used to be inconceivably different. I used to have a career that would be seen as prestigious and lucrative. I used to own a London flat that would be perceived as tasteful and opulent. I used to sleep with women who would be classed as attractive and sophisticated.

But I gave it all up. I gave that *life* up, quite willingly. Once I'd made the decision, I did it swiftly, mercilessly, without regret or hesitation. Even now, I marvel at how easy it was to transform my life utterly – how easy it is for *everyone* to transform their lives utterly. It's only the decision that's difficult.

Why did I do it? To pursue a different dream: a dream of simplicity, parsimony, feline self-containment. Once a dream gets hold of you, it rarely lets go. And to a large extent, that dream has been realised.

Do I miss the glitz and glamour of metropolitan life? Not a bit of it. I have no desire to return to a big city, least of all London – the most overrated city in the world. Londoners think their city is the centre of England, the pulse of Europe, the axis of the planet. They think London is the hub, the place to be, the funky centre of gravity.

But they're deluded. Nothing happens in London. People get up, they go to work, they return home. That's it. Londoners are too exhausted to do anything interesting; the treadmill of the city grinds the life out of them. And perpetual fear is a draining emotion: how many times can you sit on the Underground, shitting yourself, eyeing other people's rucksacks? London, to me, is a void, a vacuum. Whatever you're looking for, you won't find it there (unless you're looking for poverty, celibacy, loneliness, depression; I hope Dick Whittington packed his Prozac).

No: fuck London. If you want life, if you want intrigue, if you want *possibilities*, come out here – to the provinces. This is the real England, where ninety per cent of the English live. This is the place to be. This is where the action is.

2

AT FIRST GLANCE, IT LOOKS like any car park anywhere in England. In fact, it looks like any car park anywhere at all. It serves a supermarket chain that anybody living in England will have heard of. You've probably shopped in one yourself.

But what makes the car park English is not what's beside it (the chain of supermarket has spread to mainland Europe), but what's above it. I don't mean the sky, clouds, God, Heaven; there's nothing English about those – no richer air exposed, no richer rain concealed. I mean those tall spindly objects that rise above the tarmac. Those tall spindly objects that look like street lights.

Look like street lights, because they're not street lights: they are, in fact, surveillance cameras. You probably wouldn't notice them – they're designed to be inconspicuous. And even if you did notice them, you'd probably ignore them anyway. If somebody, somewhere, is watching you, what difference does it make? If you're not doing anything wrong (as the argument goes), why should they worry you?

That, in itself, is an English attitude. We're so accustomed to being watched, we barely notice. And when we do notice, we barely care. Surveillance cameras aren't unique to this country, far from it; but their number, their *density*, is. As everybody knows, we're the most watched population on

Earth. England is the surveillance capital of the world. There's now a surveillance camera for every fourteen citizens in this country – and counting. How long before that ratio is one for every ten? One for every five? One for every two? How long before there's a surveillance camera for each of us? Your own guardian angel. Your own glazed sentinel. Your own private nemesis.

But not everyone is so blasé about surveillance. I'm not so blasé about surveillance. Surveillance makes a big difference to me; my social life depends on it. Some people are defined by their jobs. Others are defined by their leisure activities. I am one of the latter.

I turn the key in the ignition: the engine barks into life. Reversing out of the parking space, the car feels sluggish. The boot is loaded up with shopping: my parents, despite their ages, both have leonine appetites. I drive slowly to the exit, following the painted white arrows on the tarmac.

I pass a busy corner. Boys are jumping over piles of bricks on skateboards. Others are playing football with an empty Coke can (I spot the word 'Rooney' on the back of an England shirt). There are three or four parked cars with their windows wound down. I see girls inside wearing hooped gold earrings, boys in Burberry baseball caps. I hear hip-hop blaring out, catch a sour whiff of dope smoke.

But it's a different corner of the car park that interests me: the part that is always empty. I'm passing it now, as I approach the exit. This is the part of the car park I know best. I know how the white lines are broken on one side. I know how the hedge hides the corner from the world. I know how petrol stains rainbow the tarmac. I know how that tarmac feels on my knees.

This corner of the car park is empty – now, at 5.17, on a Friday afternoon in April. But in six hours' time, it will be occupied. I hope to be there myself.

Why that corner? Why not one of the other three?

Take another look at those CCTV cameras: those cameras designed to look like street lights. They cover most of the car park, but not all of it. Not, for instance, the corner I've just passed. That's the part of the car park that I call the 'kennel'. That's the blind spot.

3

I'M LYING ON MY BED, reading *Truismes* (1994) by Marie Darrieussecq (to polish my rusting French). The narrator is gradually turning into a pig. Her sexuality is all that men see in her; their perception of her is shaping her very being.

At least, that's how I interpret the conceit. I reflect, for a moment, on the literature of transformation. It's an illustrious tradition, from Ovid to Kafka. Are we afraid of the idea of turning into animals? Or are we seduced by it? Do we fear such metamorphosis as a form of death (a dissolution of consciousness)? Or do we pine for it as an escape from our humanity (a return to our animal origins)? Both, perhaps. If I could become an animal, what would I choose? A bird, I think – a bird of prey. A hawk would do me. *The air's buoyancy and the sun's ray.*

My mobile phone makes a beeping sound: it's just received a text message. I look at its bluish screen:

hello
b there in 25
gareth & sheena

Twenty-five minutes isn't long; they could have given me a bit more notice. Still, at least I know they're on their way. I close my book and check my shopping list (or what I refer to as 'my shopping list'). Nine items are laid out on my bed, neatly and evenly:

One mobile phone
One iPod
One umbrella (it's April, in England)
One carrier bag
Several sheets of kitchen roll (stronger and more versatile than toilet roll)
Contact cards (cream paper, raised type, Sabon font: the apotheosis of elegance)
One banana (for energy: full of carbohydrates)
One tube of KY jelly
One box of Trojan condoms

I put all these items, minus the umbrella, in a small, dark, nylon bag, not unlike the bags that goalkeepers use. I brush my teeth, gargle with mouthwash and check my appearance in a full-length mirror. I look rather nice; in fact, I look rather dapper. Above all, I look *clean*. I'm wearing black linen trousers and a white long-sleeved shirt. My hair is freshly washed and tipped with wax. My Hush Puppy shoes are lovingly polished. I put on the matching jacket. I twirl the black umbrella in my hand, like Quentin Crisp, looking, in the mirror, every bit the English civil servant.

It's 10.49 p.m. My parents have both gone to bed. I tiptoe through the darkened house. Floorboards creak beneath my feet. I pass our cat, Samuel, lying in his heated basket. He blinks at me suspiciously, his eyes cracked emeralds. Samuel knows everything. Cats do. This is the chief characteristic that distinguishes them from dogs, who know nothing.

I close the front door as gently as I can. It clicks snugly – as snugly as my plans. I walk along the garden path and slip through the gate; it squeaks briefly. I glance up at my parents' windows: unlit.

I'm in business.

4

I'M WALKING ALONG A dew-wet pavement. The night streets are delicious. I notice, immediately, the extraordinary stillness. The sky is blank and starless.

I've always loved strolling – the gastronomy of the eye, as Balzac put it. I pass beneath an apple tree, its white blossoms translucent in the street light. The tree looks like a spherical burst of flowers: an explosion of petals, frozen in time. As I walk beneath its branches, the blossoms rotate in my field of vision, filling it completely.

I sense a presence behind me. Am I being followed? I turn around. About twenty metres away is a fox. I watch it pad across the road, silent. The fox sees me, or smells me, or senses my presence. It stops too; it's looking at me now, its paw kinked above the macadam. It moves its head a fraction: its eyes glint silver, like two five-pence pieces. Without taking its eyes off me, it pads into the darkened bushes.

I need some music. I take my iPod from my kitbag and tuck it in my inside pocket. What can I choose as the night's soundtrack? I go for *Kid A* (2000) by Radiohead. I hear the exquisite opening bars of 'Everything In Its Right Place', treading along my spine like cool fingertips.

Strolling past semi-detached houses, with names such as 'Woodcroft', 'Cherwell' and 'Amalfi' carved into varnished placards, past Turtle Waxed Polos and Corsas, past randy-looking gnomes in flower beds, past hedges cut into animal shapes – dog, duck, cat, mouse – I feel butterflies flickering to life in my stomach. It's primarily because the text message I received earlier is from people I've never met before; all we've done is exchanged a few e-mails. I contacted them a week ago via the internet. But I have a good feeling about them. You'd be surprised how much you can tell about people from the tone of their e-mails.

I follow the curve of the pavement, looking at the sky over the rooftops. The night isn't dark any more – the closest it gets is a hazy violet-orange. I remember, with longing, the black skies of my childhood. Gone, like so much else on the planet. I refocus my mind on the sensory present. A bird is burbling from a branch above me. A police car's siren is whining in the distance.

Step by step, the road ahead of me straightens. At the end, rising like amber smoke over silhouetted foliage, is the light from the supermarket car park. I see surveillance cameras: alien probes from a B-movie version of *War of the Worlds*. Their visored heads are angled downwards. But there's a corner of the car park – the kennel – that's beyond their gaze. If anybody's waiting for me, that's where they'll be.

I check my watch: five minutes to go. I feel my senses step up a gear – to a higher state of alert, of sensitivity. My palms, suddenly, are filmed with sweat. My groin starts tingling. The first thing to check for is a police presence: patrol cars behind bushes, officers with hand-held torches, the flash of a blue light or a fluorescent jacket. But I can't see any of those things; I'm fairly certain this site hasn't been discovered by police.

Yet.

A tall ivy hedge divides the car park from the road. I head for the gap that I always use and ascend a grass slope. Already, I can see into the car park. It looks completely empty – just a mass of white grids, like police chalk lines marking dead bodies. The scene of a massacre. I must be early, or they must be late.

It's only when I squeeze through the hedge that I spot the car: a silver Vauxhall Astra. It's standing in the car park's blind spot, headlights off. I make a mental note of its number plate. Because of the way the street light hits the windscreen, I can't see whether it's occupied or empty.

With my kitbag over my shoulder, I begin the long, solitary walk across the tarmac. I walk slowly, in full view of the car. At this moment, I realise, I'm being filmed, probably from several different angles at once; my presence is being echoed in four, eight, twelve screens, as in electrical shops with walls of televisions. From the edge of my vision, I notice a camera panning with my movement. Somewhere, the screens are lighting up a human face. Fingers are touching a plastic joystick. Eyes are blinking at my spectral image.

The way I behave in the next few minutes could decide the course of the whole evening. The couple in the car (assuming there *is* a couple in the car) are first-timers. This means they'll be easily intimidated. I have to be as tentative as possible. It's not unlike nature cinematography: you can't just charge in without scaring off your subject. You have to let them relax with you, get used to your presence.

I approach a street light and lean against it. I'm about thirty metres from the car, directly facing its windscreen. If anyone is in the car, they'll have a clear view of me now. This will let them decide whether they like the look of me. Whether they think I'm the kind of man they could do this with. Or not.

I wait for a minute, leaning against the metal. A car passes the supermarket, its wet tyres fizzing on the road. The CCTV cameras cast shadows on the tarmac. The air smells of honeysuckle and carbon monoxide. Deep in the night, I hear the screeching sound of cats fighting.

5

THEN, A DEVELOPMENT: a light goes on inside the Astra. It glows through the swirly windscreen from the murky interior – small, square and blue-coloured. It looks like the panel of a mobile phone, only it's moving from side to side, like a waving hand. At least I know there's someone *in* the car.

But what does the light mean? Am I being greeted? Am I being rejected? Am I about to receive a call or a text message? I take my mobile from my kitbag and look at its panel: blank. I look up again at the car's windscreen: the blue light has vanished. Was I hallucinating? Did I imagine it?

I remain against the street light, motionless. Sometimes, the more you force a thing, the less likely it is to happen.

I wait. One minute passes. Three minutes. Five. Nothing.

Then, another development: the kind of development I've been waiting for; the kind that makes this game of chess seem worth it; the kind that tells me I won't be leaving the car park empty-handed – the car's interior light comes on. It casts a sulphuric glow over the seats and dashboard. I can see two figures inside: a man and a woman. The man has a shaved head, the woman has light brown hair. I can't make out their faces, but they both look Anglo-Saxon.

Again, I wait. I remind myself that they're novices. Things must happen at a pace of their choosing, not of mine.

This is a critical hiatus. This is as far as many people get –

sitting in their cars, fully clothed, knowing they're the centre of attention. This is the point at which many drive off; they simply can't shoulder the burden of expectation. It's the equivalent of, say, *thinking* you could star in a porn film, only to realise – as you stand in front of a camera, naked, about to have sex with someone you don't know and fancy even less, while gum-chewing crew members hustle around you – that you can't go through with it. Or, to put it baldly, it's the moment you distinguish between fantasy and reality. To have a fantasy is easy – a cinch. Turning it into reality is something else. It takes a certain neural wiring, a special mental strength.

Which this couple clearly possess. After several minutes of what looks like nervous conversation, they start kissing. They begin gently, uncertainly, like teenagers. But it isn't long before their kissing becomes more passionate. It occurs to me that they might have talked – or fantasised – about doing this for some time. Now that they are, their excitement is overtaking them.

But even as their kissing becomes harder, more animated, they don't turn off the light. This tells me that they've learnt the key semiotic: leaving the light on means they want to be watched. How these recondite codes become known, even to first-timers, I couldn't say – it's not as if they're written down in books. But become known they do, whether through intuition, trial and error, websites or word of mouth.

Still, I wait. You mustn't approach a couple too early. I've seen this happen countless times before. A couple arrives in a car and no sooner have they parked than they're surrounded by six, seven, eight men, all unzipping themselves. What usually happens next is that the couple – who've barely had time to cut the engine, let alone do anything else – feel unnerved and intimidated, and quickly drive off. Such adverse reactions are often female-led: the woman worries that she's going to get groped by everyone at once, from all sides, in what's known on the circuit as a 'Mongolian cluster' (one wonders what goes on in the car parks of Ulan Bator). And she's probably right.

The headlights flash once (*you may approach*). Immediately, I leave the street lamp. As I walk, I see that the couple are still kissing. Their hands are out of view beneath the dashboard, but their shoulders and arms are flexing. They must be getting up to something down there.

Halfway between the street light and the car, I stop. The woman's head disappears into the man's lap. He looks down, then, with his left arm, reaches round towards her back. Once or twice, her head bobs up and down above the dashboard. When her hair reflects the light, I realise it's fairer than I thought. Dirty blonde, perhaps.

She changes position, kneeling in her seat and bending towards his groin in the manner of someone on a prayer mat. Her bottom is forced into the air, where it brushes the window of the passenger door. Her skirt is bunched up around her waist. I have a side-on view of her thighs and buttocks: shapely and firm. She's wearing a black G-string, which is tugged to one side from between her cheeks.

I want to unzip myself, but it's too early. Besides, I'm on the move again. I approach the car at an angle, so that I'm nearing the passenger window: it neatly frames the woman's buttocks. I've disappeared, now, from the eyes of the surveillance cameras. Fallen off the edge of their world.

I'm just metres from the woman's cheeks. They're more expansive than I'd thought: lumpier, more ovoid. But then, the human body is an imperfect instrument, mine included.

I unzip my fly. The man is looking into his lap as the woman continues her work. He's watching her closely; I suspect he gets as much pleasure from watching – and knowing that I'm watching him watching – as from the physical sensation itself. I examine his bowed head: it isn't shaved, as I'd thought from a distance. I can see now that the man is bald. His head tips back, revealing his face. His eyes are closed, his wet lips parted. That's when I realise: the man is not young. In fact, I'd place him in his early sixties. My eyes dart to the woman's hair: it's not light brown, as I'd first thought, and it's certainly not blonde. I can see close up that her hair is grey. Not the pure grey of the true octogenarian, but the milky, vanilla-tinged grey – like porridge with custard stirred into it – of a sixtysomething who was blonde until middle age.

I gulp back my shock. I do an impromptu assessment. I have two options:

1. To see the scene through to its natural conclusion (whatever that may be).
2. To zip up my flies and make a swift, courteous, enigmatic exit.

I quickly rule out 2. It has a knee-jerk appeal, I admit, but it would be cruel in the circumstances. The couple in front of me might have taken weeks, months, even years, to build up to this. At their age, it requires even more courage. Their confidence is probably as delicate as rice paper. For me to walk away now would be to confirm their fears, compound their insecurities. And I don't want to be the man to do that.

Besides, I have a hard-on now.

So I stay where I am, motionless. I have my hands in my trouser pockets, as if I'm standing on a blustery touchline, watching a school football match. The man reaches round to massage the woman's buttocks. He gives them a sharp smack; they quiver together, twin white blancmanges. His hand leaves a red mark on her pallid skin: a panda's paw-print. Her head is bobbing up and down. The longer I watch, the weaker my shock at their ages. I take myself out of my trousers; I'm hard and hot. The April air feels cool on my tip.

The man reaches for a switch. The passenger window slides halfway down (*you have permission to touch*). I step forward and put my left hand – my right is around my penis – through the space. My fingers make contact with the woman's buttocks: cool, squidgy, babyishly soft. They're the oldest buttocks I've ever played with. But they feel good to my touch. I take hold of her G-string and tug it gently upwards, as high as it will go between her sagging cheeks. She moans.

I hear a whirring hum. The electric window is being lowered fully (*we'd like you to participate*). There's nothing, now, between me and the woman's bottom except moist spring air. I bend towards the open window so that my face is where the glass would be. My lips are just centimetres from her rump. I think of *The Miller's Tale*, then banish the thought. I blink past her flesh into the gloomy car.

'Hello?'

It's strange to hear my own voice in the silent car park. It sounds disembodied, as if it's come from a fourth party.

'Do you want to join us?' asks the man. His voice is middle class, educated. It has the willed steadiness of someone who is deeply excited. I decide to go for broke. Fortune favours the brave.

'Can I fuck her?' I say.

He swallows back his nervousness. 'Why don't you ask her?'

I look at the grey-haired old woman. 'Can I fuck you?'

She takes the man's penis from her mouth just long enough to say, 'If you're safe,' before packing it in again. She has the authoritative voice of a midwife or a headmistress. Christ: she's serious. I was expecting a handjob at most. I'd better get cracking before she changes her mind.

I take a condom and lubricant from my kitbag. With trembling fingers, I roll the condom on. The chemical smell evokes a memory of my first time, when I was eleven. I smear some jelly over the bumpy latex.

'May I?'

The woman makes a noise that sounds like 'og-agh' – that is, a noise that sounds like a woman saying 'okay' with a penis in her mouth.

I take hold of her waist and tug her firmly backwards. Her weighty cheeks rest on the door frame; they're pale and globular, pocked with cellulite. My penis bobs at the root. The man in the car is watching us intently.

I hold myself in my right hand; I keep my left around her slack-skinned waist. I move my penis towards her, although I don't know where I'm aiming it. I'll tuck it beneath those copious cheeks, hoping to hit the right spot.

I move it around, prodding and probing. Her flesh is warm and soft.

Eventually, I find her opening (or *an* opening, at least). I grip her waist and push gently: I feel the muscles give around my width. The woman lets out a groan. I give her time to object – but she doesn't, so I push in some more. And some more. And some more: until I'm in her up to the base. Her doughy cheeks are squashed against my groin. Through the condom, I feel her warmth.

I begin sliding in and out. The man's eyes are fixed on the woman's bottom and on my groin moving behind it. His pupils are dilated. They look like five-pence pieces, painted black: the opposite of the fox's.

As I find my rhythm, I look down at the woman in front of me: at her tyre-like waist, her mountainous white buttocks. She's still fellating her partner. Her grey hair was neatly styled when the evening began – it resembled an IKEA lampshade – but with the repeated movement of her head, it's grown increasingly dishevelled. It now twists away from her scalp in wild, wispy, electrified tendrils. From where I'm standing, she looks like Albert Einstein in his late, mad-professor phase.

I think – what a good title for a book: *Fucking Albert Einstein*. Or the even more irreverent: *Buggering Albert Einstein*.

No, they're not quite right. To write a bestselling science book these days, you need a two-part title, divided by a colon. The first is the quirky, eye-catching part; the second is the serious, business-meaning part. So we need something like:

Fucking Albert Einstein: The Paradigm Error of General Relativity. Or even: *Buggering Albert Einstein: A Complete Revision of Quantum Mechanics.*

A glint in the darkness disturbs my thoughts. At first, I think it's the eye of a fox. Then I realise that the light is blinking. Is it a miniature torch? Is there a policeman in the bushes? Are we about to get stung? My heart gives a *whump!* I'm on the verge of pulling out and zipping myself up when I realise it's light reflected off a silver watch. I look harder: the watch is moving. It's on a wrist that's moving, which is on a hand that's moving, which is on an arm that's moving ...

So: we have an audience. As my eyes adjust to the darkness, I realise there are three men near the hedge. I can't see their faces. They're standing about a metre apart, their right arms moving evenly like a machine's mechanical parts. One of the men grunts; the man in the car hears him. He looks past me and the woman towards the hedge. He squints, unable to see through the gloom. But then the three figures must take shape: I see his expression changing, the realisation forming on his face.

The pace is picking up. The man in the car starts moving his hips up and down, meeting the woman's mouth in rhythm with her bobbing. He's clearly enjoying being the centre of attention. There are so many exhibitionists in the world, and so few who know it – until they try something like this. The woman senses something has changed. She lets the man's penis slip from her mouth – it slaps against his belly with a wet smack – and turns to look behind me. For the first time, I see her face: round, tanned, blue-eyed, wrinkled. I'd say she's in her early sixties. She was probably pretty when she was younger – I can still see the girl's face buried in the old woman's. Lipstick is smeared from the corner of her mouth. She blinks into the dimness. Her expression changes too as she realises what's out there. She turns and takes the penis back in her mouth; the man lets out a gasp. She didn't meet my eyes for a moment, I noticed.

My pace has picked up too. I'm going at her now with more freedom, more vigour. She's moaning with every stroke.

Behind me, I hear a long groan. No, it's more like a croak – followed by a sound like wallpaper paste being flicked on to an anorak. I wonder if it was the woman's glance behind her that did it. Perhaps once he realised that she knew he was watching her, the man was given added impetus? (Try translating *that* sentence into a foreign language.) Ah, who knows. Who knows in this Russian doll of voyeurism – this kinky hall of mirrors.

From the gloom, I hear another groan. Here we go, then. It's often the way: there's a tacit understanding that everyone holds out for as long as possible in the vain hope of achieving the group-sex holy grail of Simultaneous Orgasm. But it never happens. Someone always comes first; someone *has* to come first. We couldn't all hold back indefinitely (although that doesn't stop us trying). When someone does finally give out, it often sparks off everybody else in a kind of Mexican Orgasm.

In fact, I think the woman might be next: she's panting now with bovine depth and volume. Her muscles are clenching me off. I concentrate on getting closer myself. Being first to come isn't great, but being last to come is worse. Someone behind me gasps: there goes the third. The man in the car is pumping his hips up and down so that his jeans leave the seat. His face is starting to contort. He has the expression that men have when they're on the verge of orgasm: as if they're about to burst into tears. It'll soon metamorphose into the expression they have just afterwards: as if the pain of a stubbed toe is wearing off. He pumps his hips a final time and let's out a cry, like someone getting an arrow in the neck. The woman is backing on to me; I'm meeting her with every stroke. I feel a spasm ripple through her muscles. And then she comes (or pretends to come: I take nothing for granted) in sharp, jerking, hip-centred movements.

In the meantime, I've been working myself up. I feel that delicious, familiar ache in my groin – pain and pleasure in perfect equilibrium – which takes me back to climbing the ropes in PE class. No matter how many times I feel this ache, I never get tired of it; there are so few human pleasures to compare. As my eyes roll back, my gaze drifts upwards – to the cameras, the street lamps, the cracked, moonlit clouds.

I hear myself gasp in the darkness.

6

THE MEN WHO WERE WATCHING US trickle into the night. I never did see their faces. I wonder if they were contacted by e-mail and text message, the way I was, or whether they came here by chance. It doesn't really matter. What matters is that they behaved themselves impeccably: they gave us plenty of space and didn't try to participate, uninvited.

I exchange a few words with the couple before they drive off. We're polite, awkward, wary of eye contact. Sex is a trance that orgasm shakes us out of. Afterwards, everything is different. The woman says they'll be in touch. They have plenty of friends, she tells me, who are active on the circuit; there's one couple in particular they'd like me to meet. I nod, smile, but remain non-committal. In my post-orgasmic clarity, I've decided that they're a little too old for my tastes. I have my contact cards with me, but I don't give them one. For this, I feel guilty – though not guilty enough to wish I had.

I watch their silver Astra drive across the tarmac. It turns out of the car park, its brake lights burning the darkness.

I stand in the corner, alone. Everything is stillness. The entire encounter lasted less than an hour. Now it's difficult to believe that it happened at all. The night has been taken back by the foxes.

I hope you weren't shocked by the crudity of the dialogue.

Conversations on the circuit are always no-nonsense. It's a reaction, I think, to the euphemistic language of 'normal' seduction situations ('Do you come here often?', 'Would you like to come in for coffee?') with which one rapidly loses patience in adulthood. What we do here is sex stripped of inhibition. Sex cleared of cultural clutter. Sex laid bare.

Instead of walking back across the car park, I cut through the ivy hedge. The men who were watching us have beaten another gap through it. This will enable me to avoid being caught on camera again. It's always best to keep CCTV exposure to a minimum. If I'm filmed crossing the car park, then recrossing it after an hour, someone might get suspicious. One phone call later and there's a police car parked across the entrance every night. This has happened to countless sites around the country. Contrary to popular belief, the police are not stupid.

I tread down a grass slope on to the glistening pavement. I turn round to check that I'm not being followed: all clear. I look at my watch: 11.52 p.m. I'll be home by 12.05, in bed by 12.15, asleep by 12.30.

It's started drizzling; I open my black umbrella. I look like an ad executive or a City lawyer. In my other hand, I'm holding a carrier bag emblazoned with the logo of the supermarket chain whose car park I've just visited. Inside are a knotted condom, its torn silver wrapper, a banana skin and some soiled sheets of kitchen paper. I drop the bag into a bin I pass.

Now, I have everything I need: the night, the drizzle, my thoughts, my company. I also have my iPod. I insert my headphones and choose *Eine Kleine Nachtmusik* (1787): an apposite choice, if a rather pompous one.

Passing under the cherry tree, I experience an emotion that's both pleasant and familiar. It's not ecstasy, or bliss, or even cheerfulness. It's a subtler feeling – milder, more modulated. An absence of need. An absence of want. A sense that nothing is amiss.

The air feels moist when I blink. Blossoms fall across my face.

part two

tariq, marlon & lucy p

1

I'M SITTING IN MY BEDROOM with my laptop on my knees. It's ten o'clock on a Thursday evening. I'm checking my e-mail and listening to Radio 4 online. Two critics and a presenter (P) are discussing *La Vie Sexuelle de Catherine M.* by Catherine Millet. The discussion is taking a livelier turn: an argument is developing nicely between the male critic (MC), who says that the book is 'indisputably' a work of pornography, and the female critic (FC), who says that it's far more complex:

> FC: What I'm saying is that the sole purpose of pornography is to arouse the reader — to turn the reader on. So, yes, although Millet's book *does* contain plenty of graphic sex scenes, it also deals with other themes.
>
> P: Such as?
>
> FC: Well, art, architecture, aesthetics, bohemian life in Paris. And since—
>
> MC: Oh come on—
>
> FC: If I could just be allowed to finish my sentence. Since those passages are *not* written for the sole purpose of arousal, *The Sexual Life of Catherine M.* cannot be considered a true work of pornography.
>
> P: D'you want to respond to that?

MC: Well, for start, a book can't be 'graphic' — not unless it contains photographs or illustrations. 'Detailed', yes, but not 'graphic'—

FC: But I would argue—

MC: Second — and this is the real point I want to make — just because the book doesn't describe sex on *every single page* doesn't mean it isn't pornographic. I mean, most porn films these days — even now, after the explosion of the so-called gonzo genre in the early nineties — contain at least *some* non-pornographic scenes.

FC: Well, I wouldn't know about that. Although—

MC: But quite frankly all this talk of 'themes' is a red herring anyway because what defines *The Sexual Life of Catherine M.* as pornography isn't the subject matter at all — it's the language. Millet uses the *lexicon* of pornography.

P: For example?

MC: Well, you know, words for sexual organs that begin with 'c' and — let's say — a Saxon alternative for 'fornicate'.

[They all chuckle smoothly.]

FC: But don't forget the book is known to us only in translation—

P: Yes, it was translated, very ably I should add, by Adriana Hunter—

FC: So any so-called 'pornographic lexicon' might be a result of its transition from French to English.

MC: Okay. Fine. But how do we know …

My mind tunes out. I'm just beginning to ponder what constitutes a 'pornographic lexicon' when an e-mail arrives, derailing my train of thought:

> From: lucy_p@rocketmail.com
> To: shep69@hotmail.com
> Subject: (none)
>
> Shep,
>
> Fancy meeting up this Friday? I've got a new man in tow. Send me an e-mail or a text.
>
> Lucy P
> xxx

The sender is known to me only as Lucy P. I have no idea what her real name is – and I've never felt the need to ask.

Let me tell you the story of Lucy P. Lucy P is a former estate agent, Manchester-raised, who gave it all up to open a health-food shop in G——. She's thirtysomething, divorced, childless, with expat parents on the Costa del Sol. She also has an estranged brother somewhere near Leicester. Beyond that, I know little about her; and she knows just as little about me. That's the way we keep it.

We met on the circuit about a year ago. It was a memorable session. It took place in a small wood that everyone around here has heard of. It lies between a disused coal mine and a sewage-processing plant. You have to follow a slip road off a motorway to get to it. On the way, you pass hand-painted signs that say things like 'Free range eggs' and 'Pick your own strawberries'. If you didn't know where you were going, you'd never find it. Hence its suitability as a site on the circuit.

It was a Saturday night in autumn. The wood was dripping wet. Hidden animals scrabbled in bushes. The air smelt of fire smoke. I arrived at the scene late (I'd had to get a bus, then walk). The show – the sex – was taking place at a popular picnic site. There was a rustic wooden table with benches either side of it: the kind you'd see in the gardens of English country pubs. Lucy P was on the table, riding her then boyfriend, Frances, who was lying on his back. There were five other men around them, all unzipped (I was the sixth). The spectacle was illuminated by a parked car's headlights.

Lucy P had dressed for the occasion: she was wearing a tight white jumper, dangly ethnic earrings and nothing below but zip-up leather boots. She had a tattoo of a lion on her left buttock. She was putting on quite a show for the men around her, slamming down on Frances and throwing back her mane with every thrust. She was also letting out short, hoarse, lascivious cries, like a Russian tennis starlet straining for her ground strokes. Of course, I'd be the first to admit that she was hamming it up. But that was all part of the joy of watching her – all part of her consummate performance.

Now, there are some who argue that there's no such thing as a nymphomaniac; that such women, like sirens or mermaids, are the idealised creations of the misogynist imagination.

I beg to differ. Lucy P is just one woman, out of a handful I've met in my life, whom I would not hesitate to describe as a nymphomaniac. And why shouldn't she be? Let's put the shoe on the other sexual foot. If I told you I knew a man who wanted sex all the time, who couldn't get enough of women, who could never be sated in the variety and frequency of his fucking, would you be so incredulous? Would you not, in fact, be tempted to crack a joke along the lines of 'Find me a man who doesn't'? So why does the idea of a nymphomaniac strike some as fantasy, as far fetched? Does it not belong to the same strain of thought that regards female sexuality, and female sexual pleasure, as subversive? Is it not an extension of the long-held and wholly false idea that women don't enjoy sex?

Lucy P enjoys sex: we can say that with some certainty. I found out just how much on the Friday following her performance on the picnic table. Although we hadn't swapped numbers, I reached her via the internet. There's a website I always use to make contacts in the community. I posted a message for her and Frances ('Looking for horny interracial couple who were at C—— C—— last weekend'), which clicked off an e-mail correspondence between us. Originally, they told me they were only interested in meeting couples. Unfortunately, this is a common sentiment. There's enormous prejudice against lone men on the circuit. They're widely perceived – and I say this with a straight face – as perverts. Many couples refuse to meet with them at all, which is a problem given that the circuit is entirely devoid of lone women. (If it's lone women you're after, try singles bars or lonely-hearts columns. You won't meet any in woods or car parks; and if you do, believe me, they'll be prostitutes.) But a little charm can be persuasive. During our e-mail exchange, I managed to convince them of my (relative) normalcy. We met the following Friday at the supermarket car park. It was a clear, dry, frost-spiked night. I saw their Range Rover parked in the kennel. Starlight shone off its glossy bonnet. Evidently, this couple was moneyed. Those who assume that the scene is predominantly 'lower class' or 'trashy' are mistaken. There's no socio-economic type that dominates. Participants, from what I can tell, are a true cross-section of English society. Not that I've done any formal research – I'll leave that PhD to someone else.

Lucy P was polite, friendly, her accent classless. Her looks were Germanic, even Baltic: fair skinned, grey eyed, blonde haired, high cheekboned. She was striking without being beautiful, though she did have a marvellous body. Frances, who owned the Range Rover, was beefily handsome. He looked West African (Nigerian, at a guess) but I didn't ask. Ethnicity is a touchy subject. He was civilised, but distant. My impression was that he didn't want to be there at all – an impression reinforced by his behaviour when his girlfriend and I were getting busy in the back of his car.

This is unusual. Normally, everyone you meet on the circuit can't unzip fast enough. But if one half of a heterosexual couple is keener than the other, it's usually the man.

Unfortunately, it's not unheard of for women to be pressurised onto the scene by husbands and boyfriends. Thankfully, in my experience, it's rare. But on the three occasions that I have detected this dynamic, I've walked away – and I've encouraged others to do the same. I want no part of it. I've then blackballed the couple in forums and chatrooms – a better way of protecting the woman than going to the police, who view the scene as degenerate and swollen with deviants.

But Friday night was different: of Frances and Lucy P, it was clearly he who was the cooler. Instead of watching and masturbating, as would have been normal in the circumstances, he simply hung about outside, looking around or playing with his mobile, as though he were half keeping watch, half plain bored. It was as if he were indulging Lucy P; as if he accepted her desire to do this as an irrepressible part of her character – as one might turn a blind eye to one's partner disappearing into the toilet to shoot up in the knowledge that this was all part of going out with a heroin addict.

But nor did he interfere. Lucy P and I were getting on swimmingly. She was lying on her furry-hooded parka with me on top. In the cavernous back of the Range Rover, there was plenty of room for manoeuvre. I have a glacially clear memory of arching over her, supporting my body weight on one hand, and rolling on a condom with the other. She was already pulling me towards her, her slender legs hooked around my waist. I looked into her eyes: they were lucid, glazed, dilated with lust, the street lights pinpricks in their moist corneas. I sank myself in her up to the base. I love that moment of penetration – the most delicious a man will ever experience, gay or straight. It's like diving, sunburnt, into cool clear water; or falling, fearless, into a velvet safety net, only for the net to break.

I type a reply:

From: shep69@hotmail.com
To: lucy_p@rocketmail.com
Subject: Re: (none)

Dear Lucy P,

I'd love to meet up on Friday. E-mail or text me a time and a place.

I'm curious about the new man. Is he a watcher or a doer? I suppose I'll find out.

The Shep xxx

And curious I am – though one thing I do know is that he won't be white. Lucy P's boyfriends never are. She likes her men to be swarthy, exotic. In fact, I sometimes wonder why she bothers with me at all. Perhaps I'm her dirty piece of Anglo-Saxon?

Gentle reader, I can only hope.

2

I'M AT WORK. IT'S 4.24 P.M. Friday afternoon atmosphere permeates the office like carbon monoxide: a colourless, odourless gas, making everyone drowsy and unmotivated (resulting, eventually, in their merciful deaths).

Though it's always a little like this. Whenever I look around my office – at any time, on any day, during any season – I'm always delighted at how few people are engaged in anything even tangentially work related. I remember an old Serbian saying: *We pretend to work, you pretend to pay us.*

I do a quick sweep. Tony, my manager, is tinkering with his Facebook profile. Katie is having a hushed telephone argument with her boyfriend. Lee and Jason, who sit on opposite sides of the office, are ensconced in a two-player game of *Quake*. Tracy is writing an epic private e-mail (I spot the blue-and-white Mondrian of a Hotmail page). And Dave and Tanya are discussing last night's instalment of a reality TV show on which two of the 'contestants' had a vicious brawl on camera, causing the programme to be taken off air for an hour.

Tariq, the refugee, is not in his seat. He was definitely here this morning; he came over to my desk to fix my computer (it wouldn't print). He has to do this several times a month. Perhaps he's taken a half-day's holiday? By his keyboard is a book of poems by Khalil Gibran.

I lean back in my chair and put my hands behind my

head. Ah, offices. Concentration camps of the soul, as Bill Broady put it (in *Swimmer*). Actually, I've never minded them (offices, that is). In a way, they're miracles of uniformity. To have created an environment that's so homogenous the world over is an extraordinary achievement. Was the modern office a foretaste of globalisation? I believe it was. Wherever you are – in Europe, Asia, America, Siberia, the North Pole, the South Pacific – offices are astonishingly similar: there are tables, there are chairs, there are trays, there are telephones, there are computers, there are printers, there are fax machines, there are windows (if you're lucky). Logically, uniformity of environment could only lead to uniformity of activity; in other words, those of us who work in offices are, in a sense, all doing the same job. I don't mean what we do, I mean what we *really* do – from hour to hour, minute to minute. The next time somebody asks you, be honest. Don't say, 'I'm a solicitor, I'm a journalist, I'm an architect, I'm a civil servant, I work in advertising, I work in sales, I work in IT, I work in publishing' – say, 'I speak on the telephone, I blink at a monitor, I move and click a mouse, I send and respond to e-mails, I open and close documents, I wait at printers for paper to emerge, I make tea and coffee, I daydream in meetings'. For once in your life, tell it like it is.

Still, whatever you do at work (or whatever you *say* you do) I wonder if you do this – sit at your desk, chin in hand, idly perusing the internet for messages from human beings who want to have sex with other human beings in English country car parks. There are hundreds of them out there. Thousands. Let me give you a taster:

> **Question: we are looking for our first time experience in berkshire**
> hello .. can anyone tell us where the locations in berkshire are... we are also looking for another cpl to join us .. i am a bi fem ... but str8 cpls can help as well thankx
> **Posted by: Berks Babes**

Tip: Great site in Cambs
Station road Caster quiet sheltered out of the way spot we had a cracking time there. it was our first time the wife was well into the show girl stuff.
Posted by: dirtydawg

Question: Bolton area
Hi there ... we are a very horny couple, in our 30's, who are regular swingers but just dippin' our toes in the scene... anybody know of any good sites in the Bolton area for evening fun during the week... we love to watch and be watched!! PLEASE get in touch if you can help... See you soon!x
Posted by: 2Beavers

Tip: Identification at gatherings
How about using newspapers to identify who is into whatever? I suggest Daily Mirror 4 those who like 2 be watched, Indie-Pendant 4 single gay blokes (!), the Observer 4 those who like to watch, and Exchange & Mart 4 swappers...anyone else got newspapery ideas here? Its a start!!!
Posted by: XTC

Question: How do I start this Stateside?
I just heard about this going on in the U.K. on the news.Sounds like so much fun!! How would a guy get something going in the U.S. ???? where do I start?? You Brits seem to have all the fun!! :)
Posted by: Casey G

None of these postings really tickles my fancy. It doesn't matter; I'm just browsing. Sometimes, it's good to go window-shopping. Besides, I'm meeting Lucy P tonight, plus her new boyfriend. I'm waiting for her to text me a time and a place.

Of course, you might assume that surfing such websites at work is risky given the transparency of a computer's internet history. But I've got it covered. You see, I'm on excellent terms with the guys (and it usually *is* guys) in the IT department. They let me get away with everything, although nothing is ever said

– we're discreet, masculine, laconic. Wherever you work, whatever you do (or whatever you *say* you do), it's always worth getting in with the guys in the IT department. They'll save you untold hassle; one day, they might even save your job.

I click on a lozenge at the foot of the screen: my Hotmail page snaps up. I have a new message:

From: marlonman@yahoo.co.uk
To: shep69@hotmail.com
Subject: meet?

shep

do you want to meet me and the missis some time soon? were free this weekend if you like. Drop me a line

Marlon

'Missis' (*sic*) is a sardonic figure of speech. He doesn't really mean his wife (although he does have one): he means his girlfriend, Bianca. Bianca is twenty-three, peroxide haired, bottle tanned – and gorgeous. She's the kind of woman who makes motorists twist their necks like barn owls and career into bollards. When she's not driving with Marlon around the fields and car parks of Middle England, she's lap-dancing at Spearmint Rhino in Birmingham. Apparently, that's also where they met.

Now, for your average punter, getting a date with a lap dancer is well nigh impossible, especially when she's working. In fact, at most joints, even *asking* a lap dancer for a date is enough for the bow-tied gorillas to throw you out. But then, Marlon isn't your average punter.

Let me tell you the story of Marlon. Marlon (which, ironically, is his real name, not the name he goes by in public) used to be in a London-based boy band. They had a number 4 hit in the UK a few years ago; it reached number 1 in Bulgaria. They then split to pursue solo careers – in other words, vanish without trace. But after a brief spell in rehab for alcohol and drug abuse, Marlon reinvented himself as a minor celebrity. He's now a radio DJ and occasional TV presenter. He's even snipped the ribbon on the odd supermarket.

We met on the circuit nine months ago. It was a Saturday night at what used to be a popular site in ——shire before it got ruined, as usual, by local police, who took to patrolling it round the clock in squad cars. It's in a famous country park and an Area of Outstanding Natural Beauty – the kind of place that features on the website of the English Tourist Board. (In fact, that might be why the police clamped down on us: too many ramblers, birdwatchers, schoolchildren, Chinese tourists.) Anyway, there was no way of getting there by public transport, so I borrowed my parents' car for the night – their trusty yellow Peugeot – telling them I was off to visit an old university chum in L—— S—— (all of which was entirely fabricated). Instead, I booked a single room in a Forte Posthouse hotel to which I intended to return, shagged out, in the early hours once I'd had my fill of *al fresco* shenanigans.

The site itself was vast: a car park the size of a football pitch. When I arrived, it was alive with activity and movement. Discarded underwear was strewn on the grass. There were condoms on the gravel, like washed-up jellyfish. There must have been twenty to thirty cars. The number fluctuated as people came and went (or came, came and went). From what I remember, there was a salutary mix of lone men and couples.

I didn't know what I was in for. You never do. The scene is too iffy. Uncertainty is part of the package. But I got more than I thought I would that night: a fuck, two handjobs and a blowjob, spread over the course of three or four hours. It was towards the end of the evening – while I was being fellated by a fiftysomething woman with a pierced tongue, dressed head to toe in a white Kappa tracksuit, as I leant against a Saab Turbo with its headlights on, and Robbie Williams' 'Angel' played on the radio – that I recognised one of the men. He was part of the semicircle of people gathered around us. His hair had changed since his boy-band days: his skinhead had grown into something darker and shaggier. But I recognised his handsome, mixed-race features. I looked for signs that the others had recognised him too – but their eyes were fixed on the woman's mouth, and on my rhubarb member, and on the point at which they wetly intersected.

Why does nobody recognise him? I asked myself. In retrospect, I think they did – they just didn't care. Admittedly, if they'd seen him in the street, or in a shop, or at a restaurant, things might have been different: they might have shouted, or whispered, or jeered, or badgered him for an autograph. But on the circuit, when a show is in full swing, normal interaction is suspended. Many people become glazed and disassociated; they tumble into a trance-like solipsism. The mood at meets is rarely one of rowdy, whooping, high-fiving hedonism; it is usually one of hushed, scholarly, reverent concentration, as in a university library or a baroque cathedral. You've left the normal world behind: the world of jobs, families, money, consumption. It doesn't matter how rich you are, educated you are, famous you are, posh you are – when you're here, doing this, you're just like everybody else. There's only one goal: gratification. To me, the scene has always been defined by this purity, this singleness of purpose. This is what creates its unique democracy.

After we'd all finished, and without saying a word, I handed Marlon one of my contact cards. I thought he might assume I was gay and not get in touch. But he did, just a week later. He was cautious at first, but grew more trusting once he felt sure – he told me later – that I wouldn't go squealing to the tabloids. Since then, we've met many times, forming what I would describe as an amicable relationship. Sadly, I never see him in the normal world. But, realistically, how could I? We have almost nothing in common. He's a celebrity who gets recognised in shopping malls; I'm a civil servant who makes his own sandwiches. Our lives are two circles in a Venn diagram that are nearly perfectly separate. There's only a slither of overlap, as slender as a cat's pupil: what we get up to on the circuit.

But it doesn't matter. However little we have in common, I like him anyway. Despite his money, his celebrity and his occasional brashness, I find him sensitive, troubled, insecure and decent. Once or twice, when he's in a 'black dog mood', he's phoned me on my mobile and I've played the role of fraternal *confidant*. I'm happy to do this. Having grown up without siblings, I have a pent-up wellspring of brotherly feeling, bursting for an outlet. I e-mail him back:

From: shep69@hotmail.com
To: marlonman@yahoo.co.uk
Subject: Re: meet?

Marlon,

Yes, let's meet up soon. I can't do this weekend, so what about the weekend after? The evenings are getting warmer – it'd be rude not to.

The Shep

Of course, the other reason I meet up with Marlon is to fuck his girlfriends. You see, even though his star has rather fallen, Marlon still pulls some beautiful women. If you lined them all up, they'd look like the cast of a lingerie catalogue. Celebrities, as everybody knows, are the demigods of our culture. Their pulling power is unparalleled. They get the women they want. And if Marlon is willing to share his women with me – and they're willing to be shared – who am I to object?

I yawn out loud and check my watch: 4.39 p.m. I decide to leave early, not least because I've amassed over forty hours of flexitime. Sometimes, you just have to treat yourself. No other fucker will, let's face it.

3

LEAVING THE OFFICE, any office, always produces a feeling in me of mild euphoria. Especially on a Friday. Especially when I know I'm meeting Lucy P later.

Outside, in the car park, I unlock my bicycle. I wave to the CCTV cameras that preside over the bike shed; I wonder if anyone waves back. I wheel my bicycle towards the Checkpoint Charlie, nod to the men in the twin glass boxes, swipe my ID card to pass through a metal gate, pass through a perimeter fence, pass through another metal gate, pass through another perimeter fence – and on, finally, to the road outside.

As usual, it's raining. Before I mount my bike, I stand still for a while, letting the raindrops pinprick my face. I concentrate on feeling the impact of every single drop. It's a period of intense meditation. Every day, I try to have at least one period of meditation, however brief. Eyes closed, I visualise the millions – the billions – of raindrops falling from the sky. It fascinates me that only, say, twenty were destined to land on my eyelids. Could God have marked them out in advance, like tracer bullets?

But the rain feels warmer than it used to. Fizzier. I open my eyes and blink away the liquid. It's raining hard, but I'm equipped for it. I'm wearing a dayglo yellow mac that covers me like a wigwam. It culminates in a peak on the top of my head. I look like a plastic duck with human legs.

I begin my journey home. Squinting in the oncoming rain, it occurs to me that the weather is like this for most of the year. For a moment, my heart aches for a time when there were four seasons, separate and distinct; when the year had a proper rhythm, a proper *narrative*.

But that's all gone down the toilet. The seasons are out of joint – for ever. Today, there's mostly what I face: a tepid, amorphous, rainy mush (interspersed, for good measure, with periods of drought). Still, at least I don't have any children: I pity the generation who'll have to deal with *this*.

Right now, I have to deal with a flood. Cars are slowing on the road ahead, their wipers going in a metronomic mish-mash. A traffic policeman is standing in front of a diversion sign, semaphoring like a man on a runway. The road behind him is entirely underwater, its chromium surface crackling with raindrops.

But the diversion, of course, is the long way round. I know a shorter route – shorter, even, than the one I take daily. I turn off the main road before I reach the policeman. I find myself in a dark, narrow, rustic lane, cycling parallel to a housing estate. My wheels are turning. Rain is pattering my mac. My solitude is exquisite. I swerve off the road, fizz through an alley, zip along a backstreet, whizz through another alley, and curve, at last, on to the street outside.

I'm instantly reminded why I never come this way: it's one of the roughest parts of town. Which is to say, it's one of the poorest. (And the poorest parts of town are always the liveliest – it's the richest parts that are street dead, deserted.) Looking around, I realise that I'm not the only person on a bike. But I *am* the only person on a bike who isn't bare chested (despite the rain). In fact, I'm the only person on a bike who isn't bare chested and wearing a baseball cap. No, let me get this right: I'm the only person on a bike who isn't bare chested, wearing a baseball cap and carrying a beer can in his hand. Most of the cyclists are teenage boys, riding around in circles or clustered on street corners.

The streets are laid out in a gridiron pattern. All the houses are terraced. Many of their windows are smashed. Some are boarded up with plywood. There are layers and layers of graffiti. Every wall is a spray-paint palimpsest. I see random objects passing on the pavement: a single shoe, a three-legged chair, a TV with a broken screen, a grimy mattress with springs poking out (that'll be on fire later). I feel like I'm cycling through a fly-tipped sculpture park or a Balkan town after NATO bombardment. In a gutter lies a naked Barbie with both her legs missing. She's still wearing that patented smile, insanely happy, as though losing her legs was exactly what she'd wanted. I've read about people who long for such dismemberment. I cycle past an old Nissan Bluebird with its window shattered. Bits of glass glitter on the driver's seat, like scattered diamonds. No doubt the stereo's been nicked. I'm reminded of a bear's paw crunching a beehive to scrape out the honey. A police car is cruising in the opposite direction. As it passes, the officers pan their heads to look at my face. I snatch a glimpse of them through the windscreen: one male and one female officer. The man was rather handsome, I thought.

I've now rejoined my normal route. I glide around a corner on to Tariq's street. I spot his house immediately: a narrow terrace with a tiny concrete front garden (can a garden be concrete?) The lower half of the house is pebbledash, the upper half is corrugated iron. It looks like a brick and metal sculpture of a Battenberg cake. By the upstairs window is a satellite dish, presumably for exotic TV channels. Tariq lives there, he told me once, with four other refugees: a Chechen, an Angolan, a Turkish Kurd and a Roma Latvian. All of them work locally.

As I ride, the streets are changing around me, getting smarter. Teenagers vanish. Cars grow shinier. Debris peters out. Pillars of sky open up between houses. The world is being transformed, second by second. I think of taking off in an aeroplane – the changing textures of atmosphere and sunlight.

When I arrive home, my parents are in bed. It's 5.04 p.m. Before you get the wrong idea, I should stress that they're in separate beds. In fact, they're in separate rooms; they've slept in separate rooms for years now. Yet their relationship seems to me stronger than ever. According to Chekhov, all marriages are a mystery from the outside. My parents' is no exception.

Although I'm in the bathroom, hanging up my dripping mac in the shower cubicle, I can picture them both perfectly. They'll be sitting up in their respective beds, slippered feet sticking out of their duvets. They'll be working on crosswords from the *Daily Telegraph* (quick for my mother, cryptic for my father), which they've cut out of the newspaper with toenail scissors. They'll be peering over their glasses as they flick, one-handed, through *Concise Oxford Dictionaries*. And any moment now, they'll start exchanging crossword clues, even though, from their separate rooms, they can't even see each other. Right on cue, I hear my mother's voice:

'Acclaimed 2001 debut by Mexican film director Alejandro Gonzalez Ina ... something!'

There's a pause. Then my father shouts back:

'How many words!'

There's another pause. Then my mother shouts back:

'Two! Six letters each! The first begins with A! The second ends in S!'

There's another pause: the sound of my father thinking.

'Hmmm,' he says, eventually. My father never says the words, 'I don't know.' The closest he ever gets is, 'Hmmm.'

They're not even aware that I'm back.

I shout out from the bathroom: '*Amores Perros!*'

'A more is what!' shouts my mother. She says it without shock at my sudden interjection, as if I were sitting up in bed with a crossword of my own.

'*Amores Perros!*' I shout again.

There's a pause.

'Can you spell it for me!'

I spell it for her, shouting out each letter in turn.

'Thank you, Jeremy!'

My father shouts out a cryptic clue: 'Pursuing stubbornly with a silent whistle!'

I close the bathroom door, even though I think I know the answer. I'm just not in the mood for crosswords.

4

SHOWERED AND CHANGED, I'm driving along a rain-washed dual carriageway. I think of the opening pages of *Rabbit, Run* (1965) in which Updike describes Rabbit's drive through rural Pennsylvania. There's so much driving in modern American literature, and so little in English. We just don't have the *scope* for it. Or the cars, for that matter.

I'm on my way to a site I've never visited before to meet Lucy P and her new boyfriend. It isn't far from my parents' house, but it's inaccessible, as usual, by public transport. So I'll just have to get there by myself. I have a road map downloaded from a website to guide me. I feel excited, nervous, curious and horny.

And hungry. I check my watch: not even seven o'clock. I don't have to meet them until eight. I deliberately set off early so I could stop for dinner somewhere. I usually eat with my parents, but I was impatient to leave home and get the evening started.

I pull into the Red Lion Tavern – a pub I've passed many times but never actually visited. Through my rain-streaked windscreen, it looks unlovely. The Victorian building is shabby and poorly kept. Paint is flaking off its wonky drainpipes. Roof tiles are missing in psoriatic patches. The windows' glass is frosted up to head height, like the glass in bathroom windows, to prevent people looking in. There's a sandwich board outside with the words 'LIVE FOOTBALL' and 'SUNDAY ROAST' chalked across it. At the top of the windows hang two large flags: a Union Jack and a St George's Cross. I'd prefer to eat somewhere else, but I've miscalculated. There's nothing now between here and the meeting place. It's the Red Lion Tavern or hunger.

I pull up between two white vans and a grey Mini. The Mini has black hubcaps and darkened windows.

Walking across the car park, my Hush Puppies printing the gravel, I spot a sign on a wooden fence: 'BE AWARE! C.C.T.V. IN OPERATION'. I look around for cameras, but there's no sign of any. I wonder if they're hidden somewhere.

When I enter the pub, nobody pays me any attention. It smells of stale beer, cigarette smoke, pork scratchings and damp carpet. I sit on a stool at the bar, looking around me. The place is almost empty. A television near the ceiling is showing live football with the sound turned off. A man in a checked shirt, whitened with brick dust, is playing a fruit machine in a corner. He's bending down like a sumo wrestler, hands on knees, neck fat concertinaed, straining to see which reels he should nudge. Next to the fruit machine, a black Labrador is asleep with its paws splayed, its chin between them on the floral carpet. A middle-aged man – bald, jowly, wiry-eyebrowed, with a face the colour of Spam – reaches down to ruffle the dog's head. Next to him is a much younger woman: petite, moon faced, oriental, wearing too much make-up. On the other side of the pub, two men are playing darts. They look young, probably in their early twenties. Both of them have skinheads. The bulkier one spots me looking at them. He picks up his pint glass and swigs from it, holding my gaze confrontationally. I turn back to the bar, legs tingling with adrenalin.

I'm startled to see a female face in front of me. The barmaid, who can't be older than twenty-one, gives her chin an upward jerk. Before she's even spoken, I guess that she's eastern European. It's not her height that gives her away, nor her alabaster skin, nor her geometric cheekbones – it's her eyes. She has the kind of eyes possessed only by the peoples of central and eastern Europe: large, round, beautifully translucent, and as blue as the blue in a stained-glass window with sunlight coming through it.

'Do you serve food?' I ask.

Unsmiling, she hands me a laminated menu. Not wanting to eat too heavily, I choose a ploughman's. I cancel the onion, for obvious reasons.

While I wait for my food, the young men who were playing darts have taken stools at the bar, not far from where I'm sitting. They order two packets of crisps and two pints of Stella. I'm careful not to catch their eyes again. Instead, I flick through a tabloid newspaper with the words 'Property of the Red Lion' written on it. But I'm only half reading. I turn the pages distractedly, listening to the two men trying to engage the barmaid in conversation.

'Oi! Slag!'

I hear them both snigger.

'Oi! ... Where are you from?'

I hear her voice for the first time. It's deeper than I expected, more resonant:

'I am from Slovakia.'

Pause.

'Th'fuck's that?'

'Pardon?'

'Where. The fuck. Is that.'

Her answer is rehearsed, toneless: 'It is north of Hungary, south of Poland, west of Ukraine, east of Czech Republic.'

Pause.

'So are you a prostitute?'

'No. I am a student.'

Pause.

'D'you take it up the arse?'

Howls of laughter.

She puts a plate in front of me and vanishes into the kitchen. Through a hole in the wall, I hear her speaking what I presume is Slovakian. A male voice answers her in her own language.

I take my plate and the newspaper to an empty table. Sizing up my ploughman's, I see that they've given me onion anyway. I peruse the rest of it. The bread is stale and yeasty. The cheddar is as dry as chalk. The pickle resembles dog food. But I tuck in all the same; I'll need the energy later, God willing.

I sense a presence to my side. I turn to see the black Labrador blinking at me dolefully. It glances at my plate, then up at me; its shaggy ears twitch, one after the other. I offer it the onion in my open palm, as if I'm feeding an apple to a horse. It swallows it without chewing and resumes its expression immediately.

I flick through the newspaper, eyes skimming the headlines. UTD STAR DENIES HE. CLIMATE CHANGE BLAMED FOR. BIG BROTHER SADIE STRIPS AT. TERROR SUSPECT HELD BY. I come to a story that stops my chewing. It happened in a town just a few miles from my own. Mouth full, I tug the paper towards me:

ASYLUM SEEKER RAPE SHOCK

A schoolgirl was savagely **RAPED** last night in the D—— area of ——hire. Her attacker was an **ASYLUM SEEKER** who had been in Britain for less than **3 MONTHS**.

The lively, attractive 15-year-old, who cannot be named for legal reasons, was raped on her way home from a schoolfriend's **BIRTHDAY PARTY**. It was her first night out for months because she was studying for her GCSEs.

She was described by her sobbing parents as

> an '**ANGEL**' who would never harm anybody.
> 'We're all in a state of shock,' they said.
> ——shire police are holding a man in custody.
> They describe him as east African in origin.
>
> *Have you been sexually abused, attacked or raped by an asylum seeker, illegal immigrant or Islamic extremist? The —— Show would like to speak to you. Call us now on 020 —— ——.*

I wonder who the girl is, and which school she goes to. I wonder, too, who the rapist is. Perhaps Tariq knows him? Or maybe someone in his house does? I understand it's a small community.

I leave the rest of my food and take my plate to the bar. The Slovakian girl is leaning against the till, arms folded. As I approach her, I ponder the general surliness of barmaids and waitresses. Presumably, any smiles or signs of friendliness are interpreted by drunken punters as sexual encouragement – so the only way waitresses can avoid unwanted advances is to go to the other extreme: to drape themselves, at all times, in leaden cloaks of unapproachability. It works.

'D'you serve coffee?' I ask, putting my plate on the bar.

She nods, unblinking.

'Cappuccino?'

I hear sniggers to my side – and possibly a whispered 'Fucking wanker'.

'No,' she says. 'Just coffee.'

'Oh. Well. One coffee, please.'

As she busies herself at the coffee machine, I slowly turn my head: the two young men are still sitting there, drinking. I accidentally meet the gaze of the bulkier one. I see that he's staring at me already. His eyes are unmoving, gunmetal grey: two small springs, coiled with aggression.

'Got a problem?'

I avert my gaze immediately; my stomach turns over. I

have a spine-melting fear of physical confrontation. I leave a two-pound coin on the bar – for the cup of coffee I won't be drinking. I zip up my jacket and turn towards the door. As I leave, I hear a voice:

'Cunt.'

Outside, in the car park, I get into my parents' yellow Peugeot. I yank out the choke and turn the key; the engine starts first time, thank Christ. As I pull out on to the road, I glance over at the pub's windows. At the frosted glass, beneath the St George's Cross, are two white faces, distorted beyond recognition.

5

I HIT THE BRAKES WHEN I spot the orange box of a speed camera – a sinister one-eyed genie, floating against the foliage. Truncated white lines flicker beneath my wheels. I wince, my eyes fixed on my rear-view mirror, waiting for the dreaded light-burst. But none comes; I must have slowed down in time. The last thing I want is my number plate photographed.

I turn into a poorly lit car park. Suddenly, I realise where I am: in the car park of F—— train station, a minor station at which only sluggish regional trains stop. There isn't much here any more: just a red-brick shell and a weed-stitched platform. It looks as if it's been abandoned or bombed out. Outside the crumbling building is a fold-out notice-board:

> Due to vital engineering work, there will be severe disruptions to all services to and from this station during the period **1 April to 9 November**. We sincerely apologise for any inconvenience this may cause.

I swing into a space at the darkest end of the car park. The gravel cracks and pings in my wheel arches. The parking lines are faded and broken, like the lines in urban tennis courts. The car park is enclosed by a high metal fence, topped with barbed-wire loops. Since I left the pub, the rain has stopped, but the dusk has thickened. I look up through the windscreen:

half the lights aren't working; their bulbs have been smashed out by stones thrown up at them. On a pillar is a yellow placard:

WARNING! THIS CAR PARK IS
MONITORED BY 24-HOUR CCTV

——SHIRE TRANSPORT POLICE

Over the sign, like a diagonal 'Sold Out' sticker, someone has written *'like fuck it is'* in black marker pen. I turn off my headlights and cut out the engine.

Waiting here reminds me of my early days on the circuit. When I first started out, I had little idea how to make contacts. Like so many novices, I would visit car parks at random on a vague, rudderless quest for action. But not one of these outings ever came to anything. It was only later that I grasped the community's size and sophistication. Once I had, finding a show became immeasurably easier, and I rapidly became a fully fledged member.

I jump violently: there's a knocking sound on the side window, just centimetres from my face. I turn to see a grubby white knuckle rapping the glass. In the dim atmosphere – a mixture of moon glow and tungsten light – the knuckle is replaced by equally grubby features. The pallid face is young and gaunt; the deep-set eyes look sleepy.

'What?' I ask, irritably, from inside the car.

The man mumbles something and gestures to his mouth. I buzz down the electric window – but only to his nose.

'Can I help you?'

His speech is slurred, but his accent is startlingly posh. 'Joohavasigeretbyanysharnz?'

I frown. 'What?'

'Eyewuzjusswunderingifyoohad—'

'Oh. No. I don't smoke, sorry.'

'Howboutabitovoodthen?'

'Pardon?'

'Somethingtweatmaybe?'

'Er, no. I don't have any food either.'

'Glazamulk?'

'*What?*'

He shakes his head, swaying, then holds up his palm in a gesture of defeat. 'Notawurry. Eyethankyouanyway.'

He turns from the window, unsteadily. As he shuffles off, I see he has a sleeping bag wrapped around his shoulders, like a frayed poncho. The laces of his trainers slither around his feet. He walks towards the station building and slumps down against a wall. It's then that I notice other human shapes hunkered beside him. In the dimness, they look like figures in a refugee camp. I see a naked white arm with a belt tied round it.

I'm distracted by a car entering the car park, headlights on half-beam. Through the windscreen, my eyes pan with its movement. I check its number plate: not one I recognise. Old and beaten up, it's a Honda Civic – the car of choice for illegal minicab drivers all over England. I can't believe Lucy P will step out of this. Her boyfriends' cars are usually smart: Saabs, Mercedes, Rovers, Audis. This must be somebody else. I wonder if news of our meeting has spread. Did Lucy P and her boyfriend post it online? Are we about to be joined by random punters?

The Honda parks opposite my Peugeot, about twenty metres away, so that our bumpers are facing. We could be in a freeze-frame image from a speed camera moments before a head-on collision. The headlights go off, fading to a dull silver. I can see two figures inside, but can't make out their faces. In fact, I can't make out anything at all: age, race, sex even. It could be two men. It could be two women. It could be Robert Maxwell and Lord Lucan. Suddenly, I feel nervous. In my ear, my pulse is beating.

The Honda's interior light goes on. I squint – then I stare, unbelieving. In the passenger seat is Lucy P. In the driver's seat is my colleague, Tariq.

My first thought: that explains the car.

My second thought: what's he doing here?

My third thought: how does he know Lucy P?

Though not in that order. These questions come to me randomly, anarchically, swiftly giving way to a dumb paralysis. It's only after my shock has faded that I marshal my thoughts. What do I do now? Do I start the engine and drive off? Do I call Lucy P on her mobile to explain the situation? Do I carry on as normal, pretending I don't know Tariq?

In fact, does Tariq know he's meeting *me*? Given that Lucy P knows me only as 'The Shep', I doubt it. I haven't turned on my interior light, so he can't have recognised me yet. There's still plenty of time to pull out. I drum my fingers on the steering wheel. Decisions, decisions.

I move my fingers to the car key, ready to turn it. Then I hesitate. I look across at Lucy P. I picture her body beneath the dashboard: her blonde downy arms, her pale wiry thighs, her small-nippled breasts, her sandy pubic tuft. I see her expression as I enter her, hear her breathing in my ear, smell the perfume of her skin, feel her teeth in my neck. The next thing I know, I'm removing my car keys and reaching for the overhead light. Sometimes, you don't realise you've made a decision until you're already dealing with its consequences.

I sit in the car, lit up. Tariq must be able to see me now. I expect a reaction from him – a whispered word to Lucy P, a certain movement of the head – but there's nothing; he just sits beside her, motionless. Can he not make out my face? Is he short sighted?

They start kissing. They begin gingerly, but quickly grow more passionate (the usual pattern). Their twisting bodies crackle with energy; their movements spark with sexual current. From this distance, they look as if they're having a fight. It's amazing how violent human sex can look to a passive observer: mutual aggression between inarticulate mammals. Lucy P's hand wraps itself around his bullish neck. Tariq tugs at her breast-hugging top. Within seconds, the top is off – I see the twin black lines of her bra straps. Tariq removes his grey-marl T-shirt, his torso hairless and muscled.

Watching them from my car, blinking in the half-light, I can't resist smiling. The last time I saw Tariq he was at work, wearing his office outfit of Burton's shirt and BHS tie, tugging paper out of a winking laser printer.

I switch off the light and get out of my car. I turn the key in the door; the central locking engages with the metal-on-metal sound of four swords being sheathed. As usual, I have my kitbag over my shoulder. I walk across the car park, groin prickling. Through force of habit, I glance above my head, looking for CCTV cameras. But there aren't any. The whole place is one big blind spot – one dirty kennel.

Nor is there any need to approach cautiously; we're all acquaintances here. Although whether Tariq has identified me yet remains unclear.

By the time I reach the Honda, the passenger door is open. I stop about ten metres away. Acquaintances we may be, but I don't want to crowd them. Tariq gets out of the car and walks round to the other side. He doesn't look at me once. Does this mean he's shy? Or does it mean he's recognised me? It could mean neither, since some people avoid eye contact when they're doing this (especially lone men, who, like men in sex shops, shuffle around blindly like penguins in a snow-storm). Whatever the explanation, he doesn't seem inhibited. In his Reebok trainers and stone-washed jeans, he kneels down on the gravel. I step sideways to get a better view. The gravel crunches beneath my feet. Lucy P has positioned herself to receive head in a classic car-sex position: the Open Door. She's reclined across the front seats, propping herself up on her elbows, looking down at her own body. Her rear is on the edge of the passenger seat; her legs are folded back towards her stomach. This will give Tariq full access to her charms.

Lucy P is wearing black mascara and baby-pink lipstick. In her choice of dress, she's showing all her experience: lightweight trainers (Puma Gazelles), a long-sleeved T-shirt (now in a heap on the back seat) and a short blue skirt (bunched up around her waist). She's avoided the logistical nightmare of trousers, uniform of the inexperienced. Jeans are especially troublesome: any woman who turns up in jeans might as well be wearing a deep-sea diving suit.

With one hand, Tariq slips off her tiny G-string; holding it between his thumb and forefinger, he slides it along her ivory leg. He does this with great finesse, as if he's playing one of those old-fashioned games where you have to negotiate a metal loop around a wire without it touching the surface. The G-string drops silently on to the gravel. It's red and silky. For highly sexed women, red is the colour of underwear.

And then, wasting no time at all, he plunges his face between Lucy P's thighs. She lets out a brief cry, then clasps the back of his head. In his badger-black hair, her fingers look pallid. Tariq moves his head around, almost theatrically, as if he's engaged in a long, deep, passionate kiss (which, in a way, he is). She hooks a leg over his muscular shoulder.

With my horn tenting my trousers, I step closer. Without exchanging a word – in the kind of silent, moonlit choreography that characterises sex on the circuit – they swap positions: Tariq sits on the edge of the seat, his trainers on the ground, while Lucy P squats down in front of him. She unzips his flies, takes out his member, grips it at the base – and engulfs it. Her head starts moving up and down. Tariq is looking down at where her mouth must be (I'm standing behind her), his expression unchanged, unchanging. He still hasn't looked at me once, which is mystifying – although I know from sweet experience that getting pleasured by Lucy P is a major distraction.

By now, I'm feeling pretty frisky myself. Inside my

trousers, I'm hard and achy. I look for ways in which I might participate. In normal situations, in which the other punters might be strangers, I would be tentative. I would wait for an explicit invitation, or ask them, politely, whether they'd mind, awfully, if I joined them. But this isn't a normal situation: I know Lucy P (biblically) and I know Tariq (in his workaday incarnation). We're all friends here. I think the formalities can be waived.

I step forward and squat down behind Lucy P. I put my left hand on the ground to steady myself and put my right underneath her skirt. I feel her snowy skin contract against my fingertips. I follow the smooth curves of her globes until I find what I'm looking for: as usual, she's warm and wet. I slip two fingers inside her; she yelps from the back of her throat. I suspect this is as much from surprise as pleasure. Not that she protests, of course. I move my fingers around as she pushes back on to my hand. Then, after wetting my thumb with her nectar, I circle it around her other entrance (or exit), occasionally dipping in the tip. Her breathing is getting heavier, albeit through her nose (her mouth is full). Slowly, gradually, with a tight circular motion, I work my thumb inside her. It's not long before it slides in up to the knuckle. I'm always surprised by how thinly these two passages are separated in a woman's body. Through her skin, I touch my fingers and thumb together.

I now have Lucy P in what some would call the Bowling Ball grip. Its beauty is its flexibility: through gentle, independent movements, you can create (I've been told) some deliciously subtle sensations. As I move my thumb and fingers apart, then bring them back together, then move them to one side, then move them to the other, Lucy P responds enthusiastically. Not only does sweat break across her skin, but she pleasures Tariq with renewed vigour.

Squatting on the gravel, keeping my hand nice and warm, it occurs to me that I can influence the quality of Tariq's fellatio. By gripping Lucy P in the Bowling Ball, and varying my finger movements, I have my own hand on his pleasure dial. Indirectly, I am having sex with Tariq. Lucy P is the medium, the lightning rod that joins us.

Somewhere in the night, I hear the sound of glass breaking.

Holding Lucy P's head in both hands, Tariq slowly lifts her mouth from him. Is she bringing him too close? I suspect a change of position is imminent. Sure enough, they wordlessly manoeuvre themselves back inside the Honda. As I look on, damp handed, feeling slightly surplus to requirements, they assume the position of another car-sex classic: the Up An' At 'Em. Lucy P lies in the back seat with her legs spread, facing forwards, waiting for Tariq to hump her. She puts her feet on the front seats' headrests, using them like stirrups. Her toenails are painted matador red. I'm about to ask them what I'm supposed to be doing, wondering how I can do this without sounding petulant, when Tariq turns to me, hand outstretched. He's offering me a curvy object, sleek and silvery. At first, I assume it's a sex toy. It's only when he presses it into my palm that I realise it's a digital camera (so yes: it's a sex toy). I look up from my palm into his face: he meets my gaze, unflinching. There isn't a trace of shock in his eyes. It's then that I realise he recognised me from the outset. In fact, he might have known it was me he was meeting all along. How? But rather than being consumed by curiosity, and brimming over with questions, I simply don't care. We're both here now, getting into it. What is there to ask each other?

'For a website,' he says, nodding at the camera.

I gesture behind me vaguely. 'What about the light?'

'Use the flash.'

'You'll get recognised.'

He shakes his head. 'We won't.'

I shrug. 'All right.'

He turns round, kisses Lucy P and starts rolling on a

condom. I put the camera to my eye, the viewfinder soft and tepid. In a single, confident stroke, Tariq slips inside her. They both let out a gasp, as if they're sliding into cold water.

As I prepare to take my first photo, I feel nervous. Any pictures posted on the internet should always be anonymous. One indiscreet photo could cost you your family, your friends, your job – your life.

But I'm worrying unnecessarily. Because, in two days' time, I'll find out that Tariq was right.

On Sunday evening, looking at my laptop at home, while my parents are in the living room watching *Antiques Roadshow*, I'll click on the link to the website he's e-mailed me. I'll see that it's a website I know well, featuring stories, chatrooms, contacts and pictures. I'll see that the photographs I took on Friday have all been posted. I'll see that they've been altered too, presumably by Tariq himself. I'll see that, in all five, Tariq's and Lucy P's faces have been carefully pixelated, rendering them both anonymous.

Or near-anonymous.

I'll look at each picture in turn, and lucidly remember taking it.

The first will show Tariq and Lucy P in the Up An' At 'Em. Stilled by the camera's flash, their bodies will resemble Renaissance sculpture – all taut sinews and churning muscles. Tariq's smooth rear will be wedged between Lucy P's thighs. The flash will shine off the surfaces of their skins, off white and rich brown, in brilliant discs. They'll look as if they're sprinkled with sequins.

The second will show them in the Reverse Buckaroo. Tariq will be sitting in the back seat with Lucy P riding his lap, facing away from him. His face will be hidden by the darkness; hers will be lit by the camera's flash – a pixelated mask of peaches and cream. Her head will be angled downwards in a pose of intense concentration, neck tendons showing, her blonde hair flying outwards in a frozen nimbus.

The third will show them in the Back Seat Mambo. Lucy P will be lying lengthways in the back with Tariq on top of her, in the missionary position. Tariq's jeans will be around his thighs (his exposed bottom androgynously perky). Lucy P will have her legs around his back, pulling him in deeper. On the static screen of my laptop, the picture's surface will quiver with trapped energy.

The fourth will see them in the Back To Front. Lucy P will be sitting in the front of the car, astride the handbrake, her rear wedged between the seats. Tariq will be kneeling in the back, taking her doggy style – roughly, sweatily, with his hand on the back of her neck. I will notice, in this photograph, that Tariq has a striking tattoo: some beautiful Arabic characters curled around his right bicep.

The fifth will see them in the front of the car for The Classic. Lucy P will be reclined in the passenger seat, angled back, her bare feet on the dashboard. I'll see the flash reflected in her toenails: ten white asterisks. Tariq will be arching between her legs, his motionless shoulders as strong as a boxer's. He'll finish all over her breasts in thick milky lashes, which I won't catch on camera.

Looking at these photos, on my own, in my bedroom, I'll enjoy them to the full. But I'll do so in the knowledge of what they don't show.

They don't show Tariq standing beside the Honda, smoking, bare chested, while I take Lucy P from behind on the bonnet.

They don't show me kissing Lucy P on both cheeks in the Parisian manner and shaking Tariq's hand without a mention of work on Monday.

They don't show me returning to my car to find the driver's window smashed and the stereo stolen, along with all the CDs from the glove compartment.

They don't show me walking to the spot where the figures were slumped to find a sleeping bag, a milk carton, an empty syringe and a shattered CD case.

They don't show my expression as I watch Tariq and Lucy P driving away together, and the shadow of jealousy passing across my face.

part three

phenotypal crisis

1

IN *THE EXTENDED PHENOTYPE* (1981), his masterpiece, evolutionary biologist Richard Dawkins argues that any animal is inseparable from its environment. The animal's genetic instructions (*genotype*) are inextricable from the animal itself (*phenotype*), which is inextricable from the environment the animal creates for itself (*extended phenotype*). Rather than being separate entities, they are, in fact, integrated parts of a single continuum.

By way of illustration, let's take the example of the beaver (the animal). According to this model, a beaver's genetic code is the genotype, its body is the phenotype and the dam it builds is the extended phenotype. So although the dam is separate from the beaver in physical terms, it is also the outer manifestation of an inner impulse – the impulse to build a dam – just as the beaver's body is the manifestation of its genetic blueprint. In this sense, the beaver is the dam and the dam is the beaver.

We can apply this theory to people; specifically, we can apply it to human character. A man's character, in the Heraclitean dictum, isn't just his fate: its effects are far broader. (For grammatical convenience, I'll continue using masculine pronouns, even though this theory applies equally to women.) Broadly speaking, a man's lifestyle will follow the contours of his character. For example, if he has a strong impulse towards physical fitness, he'll join a gym. If he has a strong impulse towards intoxication, he'll drink or take drugs. If he has a strong impulse towards sex, he'll seek richly varied erotic experiences. Character, in other words, is the phenotype; the extended phenotype is the lifestyle. A man isn't separable from his lifestyle: he *is* his lifestyle. It is the outer manifestation of his inner urges.

Or it would be ideally. The problem is that our inner urges are constantly frustrated. It's almost impossible for us to live exactly the kind of lives we want – lives, that is, that are perfectly moulded in the shape of our desires. There's just too much daily clutter to get in the way: doing the shopping, cleaning the bathroom, burping the baby, going to work. Most people have to satisfy their urges when and where they can: so they go to the gym in the evenings, get drunk or high at parties, have anonymous sex with strangers in car parks. Most people's lives are phenotypal wrecks: messy compromises between their obligations and their desires.

The question is, when does such a wreck become intolerable? When do our lifestyles become so fractured from our desires that we're shaken into action? Or, to put it in the language of the model, when does the gulf between the extended phenotype (*lifestyle*) and the phenotype (*character*) produce a crisis in the organism (*person*)? In other words, when does *phenotypal crisis* happen?

Everybody has a different crisis point; often, people only become aware of it once it's reached. When this happens, a stark choice must be faced: to endure the psychosis brought on by thwarted impulses – or to allow one's lifestyle to shift towards one's true internal landscape.

Neither choice is enviable; but then, crises are rarely enviable. And the phenotypal crisis is the worst kind of crisis – it is an earthquake along the fault line of your lifestyle and your character. Most personal crises, I believe, are phenotypal crises. You'll know about it when you have one, even if you call it something else.

2

IT BEGAN WITH A RARE JOURNEY on the Underground. Normally, I would drive from west London to my offices on the South Bank. But my car – a BMW with a motorised soft top that I could raise or lower by flicking a switch – was being serviced. So I had to suffer the humiliation (as I saw it then) of using public transport.

While seated in a train on the Bakerloo Line, my eyes wandered idly around the carriage. It was then that I noticed a copy of the magazine of which I was editor, lying face up on the floor. It's a glossy men's lifestyle magazine that everybody has heard of. Every month, it sells tens of thousands of copies.

A young man sitting across from me picked up the magazine, dusted off its cover and started flicking through it. Before I had time to avert my stare, our eyes met for a moment. I wondered, looking down at the floor, whether he'd recognised me. After all, on the inside page of the magazine was my photo: a black-and-white portrait from which I grinned smugly through my Croatian suntan and bleached stubble. Below the photo was a brief, fatuous, sloppily written editorial, finished off with a digital reproduction of my signature (most glossies begin with this type of 'From the editor' section, which is invariably the part of the magazine least worth reading). But my self-regard had got the better of me, as was usual back then: the young man hadn't recognised me at all.

After staring down at my Patrick Cox shoes, I glanced up: the young man was looking through the magazine. I picked up a tatty copy of *Metro* that had been stuffed down the side of a seat. Like a cartoon detective, I held it open and peered over the top. From my vantage point, I observed the young man, unnoticed. What struck me was the way he was reading my magazine. Or, rather, the way he *wasn't* reading it. The sheer speed with which he got through it was breathtaking. He can't have spent more than one or two seconds on any of its pages. When he reached the end, he flumped the magazine back on the floor, reached into his record bag and took out a novel instead.

When I left the train at Waterloo, I picked my magazine up. I stood still on the platform while people churned around me. I looked at the front cover, which showed a young English actress, scantily clad. Across her naked thighs was a line of footmarks from the sole of a trainer. With the sleeve of my suit, I tried to wipe the footmarks off – but they were branded into the thickly shiny cover. Cradling the magazine in the crook of my arm, I walked along the platform to the exit. I passed an overhead camera and glanced briefly into its square grey face. Underneath it was a metal plaque: 24-HOUR CCTV SURVEILLANCE.

As I rose smoothly up a silver escalator, a childhood memory returned to me. When I was five, I found a pigeon under the apple tree in our back garden. I approached it timidly, assuming it was dead. It was only when I was standing over it that I saw that it was trembling. Its eye was moving jerkily in its head, its black pupil fixing me, terrified, from within its yellow halo. I fled from the tree and ran towards the house. I told my father what I'd seen under the apple blossom. I followed him out into the garden, peering either side of his legs as he walked. I stood back, wide eyed, as he took the pigeon in his giant's hands. He rose and tucked the bird into the crook of his arm. He carried it into the house, stroking its neck with a chunky finger.

It turned out that the pigeon had damaged its wing. My father, a compassionate man, kept the bird in the garage in an empty shoebox stuffed with straw. Every morning, before he left for work, he fed it fresh water and pellets of white bread, soaked in full-cream milk.

Two weeks later, on a Saturday morning in August, he was holding the bird towards the summer sky. When he relaxed his hands, the pigeon burst free in a shimmering ball of grey and white. We watched it fly out of sight, healed, across the green strips of suburban garden. My mother filmed the moment on an old cine camera. As I passed through the ticket barrier, bracing myself for the functioning madness of Waterloo station, I wondered whether my parents still had that film at home, languishing in the loft or in a cupboard. I made a mental vow to track it down; to this day, I've never succeeded.

Arriving at the office, I realised I was late. Given that I usually arrived an hour before anybody else, this was unusual. Everyone was standing around my desk, talking among themselves. When they saw me, their muttering faded to silence. They all turned to look at me. I could tell from their expressions that I didn't look myself. Somebody asked me if I was all right, to which I nodded vaguely. I was about to ask them why they were standing around my desk, like mourners around an open coffin, when I remembered: it was our monthly editorial meeting. My task was to ask each of the section editors – fashion, features, sport, celebrities – what they had planned for the next issue. I took up my position at my desk while everybody looked on, not speaking. I laid down the magazine and blinked around me at the circle of people.

Eventually, after what seemed like a lengthy silence – which, in reality, might have lasted only two or three seconds – I started the meeting with as much nonchalance as I could muster. I cleared my throat and asked the celebrities editor, Charlotte, what she had lined up. No sooner had I spoken than I felt the tension leave the room: people smiled, breathed out, relaxed their shoulders, shifted their weight from foot to foot.

But despite the veneer of normality, my brain was zoning out. While Charlotte told me what she'd commissioned for the coming issue (calling celebrities, as usual, by their Christian names – Kate, Will, Amy, Robbie – as if she knew them) my mind was elsewhere. I was standing in the back garden of my old childhood house, the house to which I've since returned, watching that pigeon leave my father's hands. I kept seeing its grey-white wings beat the cornflower sky, looped in my head like video footage.

3

AFTER THE INCIDENT ON THE Underground, my life returned to normal – almost. Ostensibly, I followed the same routine as before. Every morning, I'd wave goodbye to whoever was in my bed at the time, drive to my office in my (serviced) BMW from my maisonette in Westbourne Park, start my twelve-hour working day (at least five hours of which would consist of meetings), spend ninety minutes in the on-site gym with my personal trainer (following a carefully concocted programme of cardiovascular and resistance work) and drive home in the evening to have a romantic dinner (with whoever) or to meet up with friends and colleagues in a restaurant or gastropub. It was a typical moneyed, urban existence – the people, language, city hardly mattered.

But beneath its brilliant surface, my life was unravelling. The first sign was that I became afflicted with a bizarre and frightening sensation – what I can only describe as acute self-consciousness. It came on, with increasing intensity, over the course of a few days. I can even remember the exact moment I became aware of it. I was at home in the kitchen at 6 a.m., preparing my morning coffee, when I suddenly realised I *wasn't* just preparing my morning coffee – I was also *observing* myself preparing my morning coffee. It was a surreal sensation. I looked down, watching my own hand spooning coffee powder into the cafetière, and thought: *I am spooning coffee powder into the cafetière*. I tried to shake the feeling off as I left home, putting it down to uneasy dreams or tiredness, but it stayed with me throughout the morning. Whoever I was with, whatever I was doing, wherever I was, I could detect a strange, inescapable, reflexive commentary on my own actions (*I am shutting the front door, I am driving to work, I am arriving at my office*). It was as if every action I performed had acquired an *ontological echo* that instantly bounced back at me. It was only around lunchtime that the feeling began to fade, when I grew increasingly distracted by a looming deadline.

But it soon came back; in fact, it never really went away. From that morning onwards, I found myself living in a state of heightened self-consciousness. Although it wavered in intensity, it never departed entirely, even at moments normally associated with loss of selfhood (*I am unclipping a bra, I am having sex with Charlotte, I am about to have an orgasm*). Previously, like most people's, my life had been a first-person narrative. But now it had acquired a mysterious, extraneous, unwelcome dimension: a third-person narrative, running alongside it simultaneously. Or, to put it less bookishly, I suddenly felt that I was stuck in a dream in which I was both participating and watching myself participate. In the dream – no, the nightmare – of my life, I'd become both actor and spectator.

I felt increasingly disturbed by the sensation. I wanted to confide in somebody, but couldn't think how to do so without sounding as if I was losing my mind (at which thought, I began to suspect that I was). Once, over a candlelit dinner in a Lebanese restaurant with a Russian girl called Katia (*I am having a candlelit dinner in a Lebanese restaurant with a Russian girl called Katia*), I tried to explain how I felt. But I could tell from her strained, sympathetic smile, and her slightly whitened knuckles on her wineglass, that she had no idea what I was talking about, and I abandoned the attempt with a face-burn of embarrassment.

Then, over a period of days, the feeling started to ease. Its departure was as mysterious as its arrival. I found, one morning, that the reflexive commentary didn't intrude with quite such power; that the ontological echo was growing steadily fainter – like a sonar signal in black-and-white submarine movies. Just when I was on the verge of seeking psychiatric help, it seemed that my sanity had been restored to me.

I was overcome with relief, although I shared this relief with no one: there was no one who had known about my affliction in the first place. At the time, the only conclusion I could draw was this: if the unexamined life is not worth living, nor is the life in which every single action is examined with merciless intensity. Life is impossible without a dash of unconsciousness – a tipple of self-abandon.

But its opposite, self-consciousness, is also the harbinger of action. I can see, in retrospect, that the ontological echo was a form of psychosis, brought on by my grappling with a profound, unconscious, personal decision. The reason the echo faded was because the decision had been made. Even I didn't know at that point what my decision was. But I would soon find out.

4

IT WAS A THURSDAY EVENING, mid-autumn. We were working late to get the Christmas issue of the magazine finished (a bumper issue, as was normal for that time of year). I was sitting at my desk with a pile of pages to approve. It was already 9 p.m.

I was staring, unblinking, at a two-page spread: a speculative piece about the extravagant gifts that Premiership footballers might be buying their wives and girlfriends for Christmas. Halfway through the article, I'd gone limp with a sense of futility.

I swivelled in my chair to the floor-to-ceiling window. Socked feet on the table, I scanned the panorama. In the dark, down below, London resembled a vast, incandescent Christmas tree. The skyscrapers in the east were a latticework of fire. On the pyramid of Canada Tower, a single white light pulsed mechanically. The Houses of Parliament were lit up amber. By the Thames, the egg-shaped pods of the London Eye glowed neon-violet. I saw tourists' cameras flashing inside, like neural sparks in the great brain of the city.

And I thought – bollocks to it. What was London anyway (what was any big city?) other than a gaping, rapacious, halitotic mouth, gobbling up the world's life and energy? What was its use? What was its *purpose*? Besides, there was every indication that it would soon be ravaged beyond repair: by floods, hurricanes, droughts, blizzards, cyclones, diseases – whatever.

I swung from the window and looked around the office. It, too, was a mass of light and energy: computers, which were left on overnight, warmed the strip-lit air, printers coiled out reams of glossy pages, paper bulged from bins and in-trays, phones were ringing via satellites and landlines, fax machines bleeped, rolling out documents, scanners whirred over dozens of photographs.

Sitting in my chair, I had a sudden, violent sensation that the office was overflowing – that materials were spewing out of every orifice. The sensation was nauseating, vertiginous.

And this was just one day. What I was witnessing happened every week, every month, every year, stretching out into past and future.

And this was just one magazine. There would be similar scenes in hundreds of other offices all over the city, producing hundreds of other magazines.

And this was just London. This would also be happening in Paris, New York, Shanghai, São Paulo, Vancouver, Moscow, Berlin, Mumbai, Tokyo.

And this was just magazines. What about the production of cars, bicycles, food, cameras, computers, clothes, telephones, condoms? How could the world just go on *producing*? Where did it all *come* from? Where was it all *going*?

I was having a panic attack. I felt my heart racing, my face flush with sweat. I couldn't bear this sense of abundance, continuity, superfluity, excess. I wanted to stop it all in an instant. I picked up the remote control on my desk, which I used for the TV on the wall above my head. Vainly, confusedly, childishly, I pressed a button on it, fantasising that I could freeze everything in the office, everything in London – everything in the whole world.

But the TV came on instead, showing a live update of a reality show in which a handful of bored nobodies lounged around in colourful armchairs, their naked legs hanging over the sides.

I rose from my desk, dizzy and sweating, and left for the toilets in my socks. Colleagues frowned at me as I passed their desks. In a moment of horror, I realised how similar they all looked – clothes, hair, glasses, *faces* even – and how similar I looked to them. Had we all been cloned without knowing it? I went to a cubicle, locked the door, slammed down the seat, and slumped back. The ceramic felt cool through my Prada shirt. I heard somebody snorting cocaine in the cubicle at the end. I concentrated on my breathing, trying to control it. With a square of toilet paper, I dabbed my clammy forehead. This was no way to be spending Christmas.

My mind returned me to a Christmas many years before. At the time, I was an impoverished doctoral student living in Paris. I'd gone back to my parents' house for a week's holiday from my shoebox studio in the Quartier Latin. My parents were spending Christmas in Lanzarote, so I had the place to myself. I had planned to have a scholarly break – to start a new draft of a PhD thesis that I was never to finish.

But it didn't happen. Instead, after a listless trip to the local Blockbuster, I ended up renting the entire box-set of *Heimat* (1984), the German historical epic, and spending most of the week watching it – lying on the sofa, in a sleeping bag, in the living room, in a festive wasteland of Ferrero Rocher, satsuma peel and Pringles tubes. My thesis didn't make it out of my rucksack.

One line from *Heimat* struck me in particular. It's spoken by Eduard, an (initially) enthusiastic National Socialist who spends much of the film wearing a swastika on his arm. In a rare moment of moral clarity, he delivers a prophetic judgement on Nazi decadence: 'Some day we're going to pay for all this.'

This was precisely the line I had in mind after I returned to my office from the toilets. And it was while I was walking to my desk that I first became conscious of the decision I'd made. The realisation came to me with both euphoria and apprehension: I was going to transform my life beyond recognition. I wanted an emptier flat, an emptier job, an emptier bank account, an emptier head. I was going to streamline my life without mercy – thin it out, boil it down, strip it off, cut it back. I felt an irresistible need for clarity and simplicity. My life was a cluttered garage, and I was going to clear it out.

Which is exactly what I did. The whole process took six weeks from start to finish (see if you can do it in less). I resigned from my job, donated all my suits to Oxfam, gave my last salary payment to Greenpeace, sold my stuccoed maisonette, and moved out of London. My most vivid memory of that surreal period is driving along the M25 in a hired Transit van, playing Sonic Youth's *Daydream Nation* (1988) on the stereo. It was as if my whole life had been building up to that moment – as if I'd finally found my *raison d'être.*

Of course, I had to give a reason to friends and colleagues for my dramatic change of lifestyle. My excuse was that I needed a career break (true enough; I just didn't mention that it was permanent) and had opted to do Voluntary Service Overseas. For two years, I told them, I would be teaching English at a primary school in rural Ghana. The reaction was a mixture of bemused disbelief and awed encouragement. For a little while after I'd left London, I'd receive e-mails from people asking me how I was getting on in Africa. I'd write back from my laptop (sitting in my bedroom at my parents' house in ——shire) with exotic tales of heroic students, multicoloured lizards, luscious mangoes and Ghanaian sunsets.

But their e-mails soon died out. People rapidly lose interest in lives that bear little resemblance to their own. Occasionally, I still hear from people from my former existence in London. I e-mail them back, saying that I've decided to settle in Ghana for good, where I now have a teenage wife, four children and considerable standing among the tribal elders.

My parents knew I was moving home and didn't mind in the slightest. Even now, years later, I like to think they enjoy having me around. I don't believe they long for me to leave; I don't believe they're plotting to get me out. Why do we assume that our parents tire of us being at home – that they weary of being our parents? For nearly forty years now, they've had this role, this function. I've come to believe it's an important part of their identity – even more so since they retired and shed their professional selves.

On my first evening back, I lay down on my single bed in my childhood room. I had nothing but four walls and four cardboard boxes. For the first time in years, I had everything I needed – no more, no less. I felt a deep sense of belonging. No, a deep sense of *homecoming*.

The dog had returned to its kennel. The beaver had finished its dam. I blinked up at the ceiling and thought: I've done it.

5

ABRAHAM MASLOW (1908-1970), in so far as he's known at all, is known primarily for his Hierarchy of Needs. It first appeared in his seminal article 'A Theory of Human Motivation', published in *Psychological Review* in 1943. Although its value has been disputed ever since, many regard it as a classic model of human behaviour. It also comes in several variations, so I won't pretend the following version is definitive:

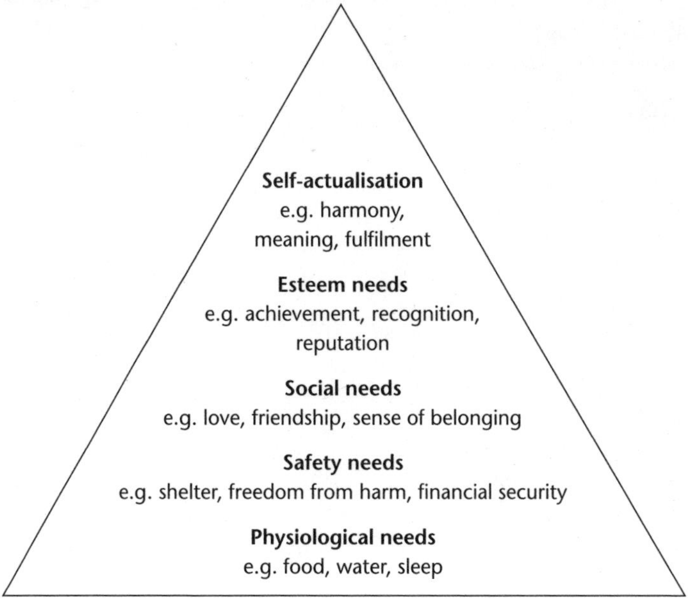

Self-actualisation
e.g. harmony,
meaning, fulfilment

Esteem needs
e.g. achievement, recognition,
reputation

Social needs
e.g. love, friendship, sense of belonging

Safety needs
e.g. shelter, freedom from harm, financial security

Physiological needs
e.g. food, water, sleep

The basis of Maslow's model is that human beings are motivated by unsatisfied needs. Crucially, it is only when lower needs have been met that higher needs can be tackled. So, for example, if the fundamental needs of food and water are not satisfied, a human being won't recognise the higher needs of shelter and financial stability. Once shelter and financial stability have been secured, a human being will be motivated by a need for love and friendship. And so on, from the bottom of the hierarchy to the top.

Although I wasn't aware of it at the time, and although the model has been fiercely challenged and criticised, I've come to believe that I was rebuilding my life in the image of Maslow's hierarchy.

The first three strata were easy to achieve: I was living at home (which fulfilled my physiological and safety needs) and had found steady, if dull, employment (which fulfilled my needs, such as they were, for friendship and belonging). The fourth stratum, esteem needs, was more problematic: after my high-flying career, how would I deal with such a drastic professional and financial demotion?

The key point is that my demotion was voluntary – I *chose* to give it all up. After being brutally ambitious in my twenties and early thirties, my ambition burnt itself out. Or, to put it another way, I came to see the futility of my achievements. Ambition, I've long since believed, is a struggle against death. Ambitious people tend to give the same reasons (or justifications) for their ambition: 'life is short', they say, or 'there's so much I want to do', or 'I just want to make my mark', or other such clichés. What they rarely admit is that, in their hearts, they think death can be cheated.

It can't. Your achievements make no difference. Death will end your life and your career – whether you're a Nobel Prize winner or a toilet attendant.

Not that I'm advocating nihilism; I'm not arguing that death renders all human endeavour worthless. What I'm advocating is clear-sightedness – the realisation that no amount of success will ever stave off your extinction. If you can accept this fact, the effect on your outlook will be profound. Once I'd accepted it myself, in my mid-thirties, my ambition fell away, and I became what I would term 'post-ambitious'.

If you think achieving an ambition makes you feel good, it's nothing compared with the well-being of post-ambition. Given that post-ambition requires you to pass through the states of ambition and accomplishment first, not everyone will reach this nirvana. But if you do, you'll see that it was worth it. You'll look back over your shoulder and perceive the ambitious with pity, amusement and sadness. You'll see them as a less evolved, more primitive species. Most importantly, their achievements won't impress you in the slightest. You'll think: *See you in the graveyard, suckers!* Nothing can compete with the lucidity, the serenity, of post-ambition. And don't be mistaken into thinking it's a giving-up; on the contrary, it's the glorious climax of everything you've worked for.

For me, there was only one problem – I fuck like a rabbit. Always have. Ever since my early teens, I've had a sex drive made of rocket fuel. This was my only concern when moving back to my parents' house. It corresponded, I see now, to the apex stratum of Maslow's hierarchy: self-actualisation. Living at home, and working for the civil service, I had everything else I needed: food, shelter, money, friendship, achievement, or post-achievement. What I didn't have was fulfilment – which, for me, meant sex. Sex, as for nymphomaniacs, is my primary source of meaning. My whole life is defined by it. This is why life would be intolerable without the circuit – I couldn't survive if I had to give it up.

But just how much sex would I get? After a wetly promiscuous life in the big bad city, I was worried that my new life in the sticks would be a parched crawl through a sexual desert.

Initially, my fears seemed justified. For the first six months, I got absolutely nothing. I couldn't even travel back to London to sleep with ex-girlfriends: they thought I was in Ghana teaching English. I finally broke my duck with a twenty-something single mother whom I met in the Rose and Crown after our office Christmas party. Her baby was crying in the next room as we pounded towards our guilty orgasms.

After this small mercy, however, my celibacy continued. Work was little help: there was nobody there I fancied. My social life, too, was moribund. For longer than I care to say, I had to rely on myself; in ferocity and frequency, I made Portnoy look abstemious. It was a dark period of my life. There are few situations more miserable, more dispiriting – irrespective of age, race, religion or income – than having little prospect of sex in the future.

Of course, Nietzsche believed that celibacy increased a man's intelligence; he argued that the spermatozoa were reabsorbed into the system, thereby boosting intellectual power. It wasn't one of his better ideas. I have no recollection of feeling any cleverer during that period. If anything, I felt markedly more stupid: my frustration was so corrosive, I could barely even think straight.

But just when I thought the situation was hopeless, just when my frustration was starting to bite, just when life was becoming meaningless, I chanced upon a news report on the BBC's website. It told of a new craze for anonymous sex in English country car parks.

And then – after months of aimless driving, despondent searching and fruitless loitering – I chanced upon another website, featuring stories, pictures, locations and contacts.

And then I chanced upon a randy failed pop star with a string of beautiful girlfriends.

And then I chanced upon a supermarket car park with a CCTV blind spot.

And in a short time fulfilment was mine. All my needs were catered for and nobody, and nothing, suffered for it.

Finally, my journey was over: I had arrived.

part four

ca-ca-cack

1

I'M SITTING ON A SINGLE-DECKER BUS, looking out through the grimy window. The sky is thinly blue, the light is thick and yellowy. On my iPod, I'm listening to *Pink Moon* (1973) by Nick Drake. I feel calm, tired and a little sad, which is how England always makes me feel. My eyes pan along the passing high street. Shopfronts shuffle past like cards in a worn-out pack: Greggs, Somerfield, New Look, TK Maxx. There's no Waitrose, Waterstones, Gap or Starbucks.

The bus slows down for a zebra crossing, its amber globes blinking in the daylight. The town centre is writhing with Saturday afternoon shoppers. Everyone looks under eighteen – or over seventy. There isn't much in between. My town has a demographic hole in it: anyone with any drive, any ambition, gets out early and doesn't come back. I should know – I was one of them.

Five teenage boys are sitting on a wall. They're all wearing tracksuits and baseball caps. The heels of their trainers tap the brick, restlessly. In their hands are cigarettes, lighters, straw-spiked McDonald's cups. I think I spot the blade of a knife; it glints, silver, in the curdling sunlight.

I watch two girls crossing the zebra stripes, both pushing prams. Neither can be older than fifteen. They're wearing baseball caps, cut-off T-shirts (revealing pierced belly buttons) and pink jogging bottoms. The tops of their G-strings stick up at the back. I find exposed G-strings maddeningly sexy; I'd rather not be faced with them. What use is being aroused in public? I can see the logic of wanting the female body covered up, as in Islamic countries (or Victorian England). Women don't get leered at and made to feel uncomfortable; men don't suffer futile erections on public transport. Everybody's happy. One of the girls is smoking, the other is speaking into a mobile phone. Her voice wafts in through the window above my head:

'So I was like – why don't you fuck off, yeah? And he was like – why don't *you* fuck off, yeah? So I was like – you're a cunt, yeah? And he was like—'

Her voice is drowned out by the bus as it accelerates. I'm sitting near the back with my feet on the curved wheel arch. I can feel the engine's heat through my soles. We're heading for the town's frayed outskirts. Outside, the passing shops are rapidly thinning out, replaced by rows and rows and rows of terraced houses, angling by in slanting parallax.

I'm one of only three people on the bus. The other two are an elderly couple, sitting near the front. I can see the backs of their heads, like the heads of two wax dummies. The man is bald, apart from a horseshoe of peppery hair around his crown. The woman has a grey-blonde bouffant, puffed out over her shoulders in gossamer tufts.

Then I realise: it's the couple I met in the supermarket car park. Gareth and Sheena, wasn't it? Although these could have been pseudonyms. Nevertheless, I'd recognise the woman's hair anywhere (that's not all I'd recognise). Around their feet are four bulging carrier bags. I look at their distended logos: Boots, Tesco, B&Q, Quality Seconds. Just another elderly couple, out doing their shopping.

The woman presses the red button on a handgrip: it makes a pinging sound and lights up a panel, 'BUS STOPPING'. Below the panel is a picture of three bags – a briefcase, a holdall and a rucksack – positioned like undesirables in a police line-up. Beneath the picture is some text:

Don't make your bag a suspect

Please keep hold of your belongings at all times. If you see an unattended bag, ask if it belongs to anybody. If nobody claims it, leave it alone and contact a member of staff or a Police Officer.

I blink around the empty bus, wondering how I would contact a Police Officer.

The bus slows down as it approaches the stop. The elderly couple rise from their seats. The man picks up some crutches from the seat behind him. I notice, now, that his right foot is in plaster. As they shuffle off the bus, he says 'thank you' to the driver.

I'm the only person left. We'll soon reach the final stop, where the bus will terminate. From there, I'll have to walk half a mile to the site where I'm meeting Marlon and Bianca. I would have come by car, but my parents have taken the Peugeot to an out-of-town theatre complex. My mobile makes a bleeping sound; I take it from my kitbag. Marlon has sent me a text message:

Shep, another cpl cuming,
last minute thing, but their cool
dont worry, c u in a bit

So: the party's growing. Fine by me. With any luck, the other guy will be one of Marlon's celebrity cronies, with a model for a wife or a girlfriend.

As I put my phone away, I have a thought that freezes my hand on the kitbag's zip: what if the couple we're meeting is the elderly couple who've just got off the bus? I wonder, again, what was in those carrier bags. Maybe they didn't contain prunes, vitamins, creosote for the shed. Maybe they contained lubricant, butt plugs, pants to cut the crotches out of.

Fuck it. Who knows? Who knows *what's* in people's bags? For all they know, I could be carrying a severed head.

The bus pulls up at its final stop. The vehicle shudders to

stillness, like a dog shaking out its coat. The driver yells, 'All change please!' from his air-holed glass box. I step off and say 'thank you' to him. 'You're welcome, sir,' he chirps back. The last (and only) time I said 'thank you' to a bus driver in London, he looked at me as though I'd asked him if he liked choirboys.

Once you've left the bus, there are only two directions in which to walk: back towards the final row of terraced houses, or forward along an A-road into birdsung countryside. Almost everyone, I imagine, walks back towards the houses. With my white headphones in my ears, and my black kitbag over my shoulder, I set off along the road.

As I walk, sky and fields open up ahead of me. The grey-white cloud looks like the flank of a tiger shark. I can feel the driver's eyes on my back, hear his brain making a note of my appearance, ready to phone it in to *Crimewatch*: 'He was about six foot one, late thirties, short brown hair, well spoken and courteous. He certainly didn't look like a murderer/armed robber/paedophile/terrorist.' And the knowing officer saying, 'No, sir, they never do.'

I'm walking towards a Texaco garage. It clings to the edge of my town with stolid desperation. It's enormous. Apart from being almost a full-sized supermarket, it has a drive-through (or 'Drive Thru') Burger King attached to it. I scan the forecourt. There are two cars parked among the petrol pumps – a grey Mini and a black Suzuki jeep – but no sign of their owners.

In the shop, I buy a banana and a can of Red Bull. The man at the counter is young and swarthy. He's speaking into a mobile phone in what sounds like Turkish. He serves me without once making eye contact. Leaving the garage, I notice that the cars have vanished.

As I walk beside the road, the wind buffets my face. It brings with it the smells of the countryside: grass, leaves, manure, flowers. I see a tithe barn in a field ahead of me. A church steeple spikes the horizon. In the sky, a kestrel hovers above a grassy mound, riding the air, wings flickering – a rebel humming bird, expelled from paradise. I stop for a moment, stunned by its beauty. It's suspended in the air, like a mobile from a ceiling. It tucks in its wings and plummets, missile-sleek.

I'm heading for a car park at a remote picnic spot. It's at the top of a hazy promontory, overlooking farmland. It used to be a popular site until police got wind of it. Now it has a reputation for being unsafe. I've read several chatroom postings warning of a police presence. But I also know that, if they still patrol it at all, they'll only do so at night. I check my watch: 5.46 p.m. At this time, I'd have more chance of being seen by a rambler or a hang-glider than by Plod with a torch and a doughnut. There aren't many sites that are safer in daylight than in darkness: but this is one of them.

I reach the car park and glance around. It's little more than a stony area about the size of a tennis court. But it's set back from the road and surrounded by thick bushes. There are no lights and no CCTV cameras (unless they're hidden in foliage – which they might be in the future). If someone could design a site specifically for outdoor sex, it would look something like this. All it needs is a drinks machine, a condom dispenser and deckchairs for the punters.

Then I notice a car parked in a corner behind me: a Suzuki jeep. Is that the same jeep I saw at the service station? It doesn't look the same colour – dark brown rather than black – but that could be a trick of the light. I don't recognise its number plate. But while the jeep in the forecourt was empty, this one isn't. From behind, I see two silhouetted figures inside. They're sitting in the front seats, neither of them moving.

I pause on the grass. Wind pushes through leaves with the sound of tide through shingle. From somewhere, I hear the *ca-ca-cack* of a magpie. For a moment, I wonder whether the figures in the car are Marlon and Bianca. But I don't recognise the car. I've come to know all of Marlon's cars – an Aston

Martin, a Jaguar XJS and an Audi R8 – and this isn't one of them.

I decide to play it safe. For now, I'm just going to hide. But when I step back, trying to creep behind a bush, the jeep's horn sounds. I freeze – like a fox crossing a road at midnight. *Fuck*. The people in the jeep must have seen me in their mirrors. I stand on the spot, grinning like a half wit. Not knowing what else to do, and actually cringing as I do it, I simply wave. My cheeks redden with heat; my armpits fizz with embarrassment. But what choice do I have in the circumstances?

The passenger window whirrs down and a woman's head pops out. I'd put her in her mid-thirties. She's attractive: olive skinned, dark haired, possibly Italian or Spanish. She has a beautiful smile – all porcelain teeth and deep red lipstick.

Porcelain teeth and deep red lipstick – a delicious combination. It makes me think of Lucy P. She often gets lipstick smeared across her teeth when I'm fucking her.

Relaxed by this full-blooded welcome, I approach the jeep. The woman's hair is tied up at the back. Stray wisps have blown across her face. She brushes one away; it sticks to her painted lips.

'Hello,' she says.

Despite her exotic aura, her voice is pure England. I hear the telltale echoes of public-school cloisters.

'Hello.' My own voice sounds flat by comparison.

She offers me her hand, which I take; it's warm and dry. Her nails are manicured, as red as her lips.

'You must be The Shep.'

'That's right.' I smile broadly, trying to turn on the charm. She's a lovely creature.

'My name's Venetia. And this is Simon.' She leans back as the man in the driver's seat leans forward. He looks about my age, maybe a year or two older. He has a broad, jolly, ruddy face, not unlike a Hogarth caricature. His smile brings out the crow's feet at the corners of his eyes. His receding hair is cut close to his scalp.

'Please to meet you,' he says.

His voice sounds slightly cockney but has been smoothed off at the edges, as if he were a part-time plumber, part-time OU student. Judging by the jeep and the country-gent outfit – green waxed jacket, blue Oxford shirt, tan suede gloves – he's made a bit of money. *Definitely* a plumber then.

Leaning in at the window, I look down at the woman's cleavage: in her low-cut black top, her tits look suntanned. A golden crucifix is nestled between them. She's watching me watching; I can feel it.

'We're friends of Marlon's,' she says (at which I resume eye contact). 'We're meeting him here too. He told us who you were. He said he'd send you a text to warn you.'

'He did,' I say. 'I'm just' – I pause – 'surprised.'

The woman blinks at me. 'In a good way?'

I nod. 'In a good way.'

I wonder, on reflection, if the man is a footballer, or ex-footballer. I don't recognise him, but he might have played in the lower divisions. The clue is Venetia: she could easily be a footballer's wife, albeit a slightly ageing one. But her years suit her. Some women grow into their beauty, inhabit it more comfortably with age. Venetia, I sense, is one of them.

'So have you been doing this long?' she asks, with a willed casualness that makes her sound self-conscious.

I shrug. 'A few years.'

'Really?'

'You?'

'About two,' says the man. 'Although it feels like we've just got into it, you know? There are so many of us now, aren't there? I just wish we'd tried it earlier.'

'So do I,' I say. 'But I'm doing my best to make up for lost time. It all depends how active you are.'

'Are you more active than Marlon?' asks the woman.

I tip my head from side to side. 'Hard to say.' I grin. 'I think he's as obsessed with it as I am.'

I can feel the woman's eyes moving over my face. Oh, she's a swinger all right. It's the subtle signs that give you away, although you have to know how to read them. I know how to read them – I've had years of practice. They're learned semiotics, decoded over time: discreet, arcane, masonic. I wonder whether the man notices her studying me; and, if so, whether he cares. In fact, it might have the opposite effect: it might turn him on.

'You're not a footballer are you, by any chance?' he asks.

Great minds; I smile. 'No. Far from it. The last time I played football was at school. I barely even watch it on TV now. What do you two do?'

No sooner have I asked this question than I regret it. It breaks one of the unwritten codes of the circuit: not to enquire about each other's backgrounds. But the couple are too mild to be fazed by it.

'I'm in IT,' says the man.

'And I iron his shirts,' says the woman.

We all laugh.

I hear the crinkling of tyres across the car park. I turn to see a sky-blue Jag rolling towards us: Marlon. But it's his passenger I'm interested in.

The car comes to a halt. Its engine, near-silent anyway, dies. Marlon gets out. He's looking smart, dressed in a fudge-coloured leather jacket (Versace, at a guess), cream vest, faded blue jeans and tasselled leather loafers. A bling gold chain is glittering around his neck.

Then Bianca gets out, effortlessly upstaging him. Tom Wolfe has written of the 'kerb flash' – the shock – of overwhelming wealth. But what about the kerb flash of overwhelming beauty? Bianca is the epitome of unapologetic female sexiness; the phrase 'filthy gorgeous' could have been coined for her. She's dressed in a taut pink Von Dutch T-shirt, short denim skirt, knee-high cowboy boots and, knowing her, nothing else. Her tan looks a little orange, but she gets away with it. Beautiful people get away with everything. Beauty is nature's unfairest endowment.

We all exchange greetings, and kiss, like dignitaries. Marlon seems excited to see his friends again. The atmosphere is relaxed, but there's a whiff of urgency: we only have a couple of hours before sunset.

After a brief discussion, Bianca and Marlon agree to go first. The rest of us position ourselves in a semicircle around the Jag. Bianca drapes herself over the bonnet – languorously, like Cleopatra awaiting her grapes. She lies back and props herself up on her elbows. She's still fully clothed, which I'm sure won't last. Marlon removes his jacket and kneels down on the grass. He pulls Bianca towards him by her boots. Then his head disappears inside her skirt. Her face tips back, her eyes close, she starts moaning. Is she acting up? Is she performing for us? Maybe. Who cares? Marlon's gold necklace swings with his momentum. In pale-knuckled hands, he grips her orange kneecaps. Simon and Venetia are standing to my side. Venetia has slipped her hand down the front of Simon's chinos. At the edge of my vision, I see jerking movement.

Standing there watching, with a hard-on like a bratwurst, I begin to feel euphoric. This is a win-win situation. Either I'm going to fuck Bianca. Or I'm going to fuck Venetia. And they're both fucking gorgeous.

Or maybe I'll fuck them both? Maybe I'll fuck them both *at the same time*? Mentally, I slap my own face: Shep, calm down. I know you're excited – who wouldn't be? – but don't go overboard. Even if Bianca and Venetia agreed to it, you couldn't fuck them both at the same time – you don't have two cocks (unlike the male iguana, lucky bastard). Just take what comes your way, and be grateful for it.

Of course, what comes my way depends partly on what kind of man Simon is. What kind of man is Simon? Does he like to be watched as he fucks Venetia? Or does he like to watch other men fucking her? Needless to say, I'm praying for the latter.

As Marlon and Bianca change position, I reflect on this bizarre conjugal fetish. Why on earth would any man want to watch his partner being fucked by somebody else? And why would any woman want to watch her boyfriend or husband doing it?

The answer, I decide, is emotional masochism. While Marlon moves to the bonnet, and Bianca kneels on the grass, I formulate a theory. In watching a partner having sex with another person, we experience intense sexual jealousy – and therein lies the masochistic pleasure. But this pleasure also derives from keeping this jealousy contained. In other words, we experience the ascetic, self-elevating pleasure of conquering a powerful impulse. But what happens to this conquered impulse? (I've long thought of impulses and emotions as forms of energy; and energy, according to certain laws of physics, can neither be created nor destroyed.) It finds expression, I believe, as sexual arousal, which is why watching a partner having sex with somebody else is such a turn-on. It follows, then, that if a husband watches his wife being fucked by another man, the first thing he'll want to do afterwards is fuck her himself – in which case, his desire for his wife is actually his original sexual jealousy, transformed. The sex act then becomes an aggressive act of revenge for her transgression (to which he assented, of course), reinforcing Robert J. Stoller's theory that the real engine of sexual desire is the wish to inflict harm, even – or especially – on someone we love.

Which may or may not be true. Whatever. What really matters – right here, right now, in this picnic spot in provincial England – is that Bianca is on her knees, sucking Marlon's cock. He's sitting on the bonnet with his loafers on the grass, arms stretched back towards the windscreen. He's looking down, watching Bianca going about her work. The expression on his face is varying subtly; you could plot those variations against the movements of her tongue.

When Marlon can bear her tongue no longer, he climbs on to the Jag's sky-blue bonnet, prick twanging at the root. He chivalrously takes Bianca's palm in his, as if she's royalty, and helps her up there too. She puts herself on all fours, facing away from Marlon, her natural tits hanging over the windscreen. She holds the ridge of the roof to support herself. Marlon kneels on the bonnet behind her and lifts up her skirt. As I suspected, I see no underwear: just honey-coloured cunt and arse. He grips her hips in both hands and slides his cock inside her. His sovereign rings flash gold in the sunlight.

This, I can tell you now, is one of the most ostentatious of all car-sex positions: the Over The Top. It's strictly for hardcore exhibitionists. It's basically doggy style on the bonnet of a car, which becomes a kind of pedestal. It also carries considerable risk, especially in daylight: because the couple are so high up, they can be seen easily from some distance. Not one, say, for the flatlands of East Anglia.

Still, they're going at it with admirable relish. Marlon is fucking Bianca with a steady rhythm; she's pushing back on to him with real aggression. The countryside is almost silent. Apart from the odd twitter of birdsong, and the occasional rustle of wind-stroked leaves, all we can hear are their grunts and gasps.

After a noisy orgasm, which sends a magpie flickering out of a nearby tree in a turquoise shimmer of black and white, Marlon withdraws from Bianca, holding the condom in place. He climbs down from the bonnet and disappears inside the Jag. Bianca promptly changes position: she gets down off all fours and sits on the bonnet, facing us. She leans back on her elbows; her tanned, toned stomach is sheened with sweat. She lazily opens her legs; three pairs of eyes slide to the same point. Her pussy is pink and neat, her pubes trimmed to a tufty black caterpillar. She closes her legs, still wearing her boots. She raises her eyebrows as if to say: *who's next?* In private, Marlon has told me that Bianca is the most highly sexed woman he's ever met – which, given that he's a former pop star who's slept with Lucy P, is saying something. He also suspects that she's been in the odd porn film in Prague and Budapest, but I'm sceptical. Still, who knows? Everybody has a secret life. Or anybody interesting.

In the absence of reaction from Simon, whose chinos are still hosting Venetia's jerking hand, I make an executive decision – I'm going next. I step towards the Jag, eagerly unzipping my flies. I lower my trousers and roll on a condom. I line it with KY jelly, as if I'm striping a hot dog with mustard. I tug Bianca towards me by her slender ankles (I do love a woman with slender ankles). I stand in front of the bonnet, cock sticking out of my boxer shorts. I grip her calves and hook her feet over my shoulders, lifting her back from the sparkly paintwork. Her eyes are dilated, aquamarine; the sun is reflected, twice, in her pupils. I slip my hands underneath her and interlock my fingers; the skin of her back feels hot on my palms. This is a position known as The Bridge. When I slide inside her, I see a gratifying look on her face: her mouth opens, her eyes bulge, her eyelashes flicker. Her body is tensed, her breathing shorter. She pushes her fingernails into my stomach to control my depth.

As I start to build up a good rhythm – shirt off, trousers around my knees, enjoying the friction of her suede boots on my naked shoulders – I gradually realise what Marlon is doing: he's standing to the side of the Jag, filming us both with a digital video camera. So *that's* why he wanted to meet up in daylight, dirty bastard. He's holding the gadget in one hand, watching the show on a fold-out screen. With his other hand, he's rubbing his cock through his jeans. He spots me looking directly into the camera and moves his head to one side. For a moment, I hold his gaze – and he holds mine. Then his face, expressionless, moves back out of sight.

Bianca, too, is aware that he's filming. I know this because her behaviour has changed – in short, she's become markedly hornier. Her grunts are louder, her movements more forceful. I suddenly feel as if she's fucking *me*. Now, I've been filmed and photographed on the circuit many times, and it's never affected me – I just carry on as normal, humping whoever. But, for some people, being filmed or photographed flicks a switch inside them. This switch flicks one of two ways: either it makes them wilt and shrivel, like a delicate flower in burning sunlight; or it makes them blossom gloriously with freedom and excitement.

Bianca's switch, unsurprisingly, flicks the second way – and don't I know it. As I lean in to kiss her, I feel her hand clasp the back of my neck. Her tongue pushes so far into my mouth that I almost gag. Her other hand squirrels inside my boxer shorts and parts my cheeks. I feel a long, sharp fingernail poking around my cleft. She breaks off our kiss to moisten her finger in her mouth, as if she's tasting cake mix. Then she moves her finger back to where it was – and twists it inside. I can't help yelping.

And I can't help coming. To my horror, it happens before I can stop it. Pain and pleasure shimmer up through my groin. It's as if her finger pressed a button to release all the jism inside me.

Swaying on my feet, I feel faint and dizzy. At first, I assumed that Bianca's behaviour had changed because of the video camera. But now my dizziness is clearing, I'm beginning to wonder. Why did she do that trick with her finger? Did she do it to speed up my orgasm? Did she just want to get it over with so she could get boned again by Marlon? However paranoid that sounds, it would be natural in the circumstances. In any threesome, one partner is always preferred over the other – it's just that the preferred partner is usually me.

Still, I couldn't blame her: Marlon is rich, famous, good looking, emotionally complex, with a cock that a donkey would be proud of. And he doesn't live with his parents. Or arrive by public transport.

I withdraw from Bianca's pussy, the condom damp and heavy. I feel rather embarrassed. Marlon, who's always had remarkable powers of recovery (Viagra?), is preparing to take my place. This only fuels my suspicions of a conspiracy. Before I've even removed my condom, he's already plonked the video camera in my hands and is rolling on a rubber of his own. I shuffle backwards from the Jag with my trousers around my Hush Puppies, like a convict with shackled ankles. My shrink-wrapped prick is swinging from my boxer shorts.

In the video camera's screen, I watch Marlon approaching Bianca on the bonnet. To give them time to position themselves, I pan the camera towards Venetia and Simon. But they're no longer standing on the gravel, watching us: they're in the back of their jeep, urgently getting down to it. So: *The Shep And Bianca Show* was the perfect aphrodisiac. Simon is struggling to remove his coat with his arms behind his back, like a lunatic in a straitjacket. *Go on, my son! Give her one from The Shep!* Venetia is pulling her top over her head, her big brown jugs spilling out of her bra. I'm about to ask them to wave to the camera when I hear Marlon calling out. It's the first time anyone's spoken in minutes.

'Oi! Blood! Are you still filming or what?'

'Sorry.' I turn back to the Jag. Shuffling awkwardly, I stumble slightly on the gravel; the camera jerks up and down.

'Easy, tiger, easy,' says Marlon, laughing.

I point the camera at Bianca and Marlon: cheek to cheek, their faces fill the screen. They smile, then giggle, then kiss, like newlyweds. Except there's no church, no vows, no vicar, no confetti.

Bianca sits on the bonnet between the headlights; Marlon gently parts her thighs. She grips his shoulders as he guides his cock towards her golden arse. I press 'ZOOM' on the video camera. *Ca-ca-cack* goes a magpie. In he slides.

2

WHEN I ARRIVE BACK HOME, the house is deserted. I have a post-coital ache in my groin, warm and delicious. In the house, it's cool and dark. A single lamp is glowing in the living room. Walking towards the kitchen, I pass Samuel lying in his heated basket; he blinks at me contemptuously. Above the basket, on the table, is a framed photo of him that my mother had taken professionally: a three-quarter profile, as if he'd sat for Titian.

In the kitchen, I find a Post-it note on the fridge. I instantly recognise my father's handwriting. One of the many subtle changes I've noticed in my father since he retired is that he now writes everything in purple ink. Another is that he uses a twenty-four-hour clock. I read the message:

Jem,

We're still at the cinema. The 19.00 performance was full so we're catching the 21.00. There's a mushroom risotto in the fridge if you fancy it – give it four minutes in the microwave. One of your colleagues rang (Stacy?) but left no message.

See you later!

Dad x

He means 'Tracy', who works in my office. But why would she ring me at home, and on a Saturday night? In fact, how did she get my number in the first place? I wonder if she's active on the circuit. Perhaps she's cracked my identity from a website. Questions, questions. A tiger moth flutters to life in my stomach.

I go upstairs and undress. In the speckled darkness, I cross the landing, naked. In the shower, there's a waterproof radio hanging from the dial. I switch it on; it's tuned to a local radio station. There was a time when my parents only listened to world news. Now they only listen to local news. Their horizons have shrunk along with their bodies.

> —arguing that the installation of baggage scanners at ——shire railway stations would be hugely costly and unworkable in practice.

I start shampooing my hair. As I listen to the female newsreader, my hands slow down to stillness on my head. I stand in the shower, wearing a helmet of foam, motionless in the streaming water:

> —was brutally attacked in B—— town centre last night. The man, Tariq Gbari Abdullah, a local civil servant, was walking home after an evening out with friends when he was set upon by a group of white youths, who beat him with metal pipes and a cricket bat. In a horrific twist, his attackers also used what police think was a kitchen knife or a sharpened vegetable peeler to carve off a tattoo on his right arm. Mr Abdullah managed to escape his attackers and reach the A&E department of S—— Hospital, where he is now recovering in intensive care. Although the attack took place in full view of CCTV cameras, the company responsible for surveillance claims that the relevant footage has been erased from their records. They have promised to launch a full investigation into what has happened to the missing

data. Police are treating the attack as racially aggravated and urge any eyewitnesses to come forward.

Proposals to build wind turbines in H—— have been scuppered by local pressure groups. Far from being environmentally friendly, says opposition activist Wilfred Burton-Brown, the giant turbines would—

I switch off the radio, my hair unrinsed. I reach for a flannel to wipe my face: shampoo is stinging my eyes.

3

IT'S MONDAY AFTERNOON, 5.07 p.m. I'm cycling home from work, as usual. My day was just like any other; I couldn't pick it out from an identity parade of the whole year. The days are all the same, really. Or once you reach a certain age they are.

Although it's early summer, my face is being spanked by wind-blown sheets of drizzle. The air is warm and sticky. Rivulets of sweat are running from my armpits. I could be cycling through a Bangkok winter. Last week, the days were bitter. The week before, the weather was balmy. For next week, snow is forecast.

I see groups of boys on street corners. Almost all of them have their hoods up. A police van cruises past them, windows lowered. The van stops outside a terraced house where a squad car is already parked. A policewoman is standing on the pavement, murmuring into a walkie-talkie. I do a double-take: it's Tariq's house. I clench my brakes; they do little to slow the rain-greased wheels. I press my shoe-heels into the tarmac until I scrape to a halt. The front of the house is covered in graffiti. Over the corrugated iron, in white spray-paint, is written:

MUZLIMS TERORISTS AND RAPISTS LIVE HERE

Across the pebble-dash, in red spray-paint:

FUCK OUR WOMEN AND WE FUCK YOU

I stare, puzzled, at the second message.

The house itself looks as if it's been trashed. The living-room window has been smashed in one corner; a flap of net curtain flutters from the jagged hole. There's a smudged boot-print on the white front door. Around the letterbox is a charred black burn mark. The satellite dish on the wall is wonky. The receptor at its centre has been broken in half, like the fragile stamen of a wild flower.

I decide not to hang around: there's violence in the air, in the wind, in the drizzle. I push off on my bike, head down. Cars sear past me, throwing up arcs of grimy rainwater. But instead of continuing straight home, I turn left down a shaded B-road. I pass a vandalised sign: 'HOSPITAL'.

In the car park, I D-lock my bike to a lamp-post. Attached to it is a placard: 'WARNING! CCTV IN OPERATION'.

At reception, I tell the nurse I've come to visit Tariq Gbari Abdullah. She looks him up on her computer, her delicate hand moving the plastic mouse. Her index finger cracks the mouse's back; her cuticle moons are round, chalk-white. She looks up at me, blinks, and gives me his room number in inflected English.

In the lift to the third floor, I wonder if Tariq will even be able to speak. I hear again the newsreader's voice, as smooth as the voice of an air stewardess, as though she were offering duty-free at thirty thousand feet, rather than describing an attack with a kitchen knife.

When the lift doors rumble open, I see him immediately. He's in intensive care, in a small ward of six. The other beds are empty. He has machines all around him: lights, tubes, wires, dials. No cards, no grapes, no flowers, no relatives. His face is turned towards the window, his eyes closed, their lashes long and dark. Through the blank expanse of glass, the sky is the colour of recycled paper.

I look along the corridor in both directions. At one end, in the distance, a big-hipped nurse crosses the mint-green floor. She doesn't see me. The door whumps shut on its automatic hinge; the sound bounces off the polished surfaces. The second door does the same.

Silence.

When I turn back to Tariq, he's staring at me, blinking. He looks confused, as if I were an obscure relative who's travelled across Europe to visit him. He probably doesn't know whether he's awake or dreaming. Nor do I, half the time.

Then I remember: I'm still wearing my tent-like yellow mac and bicycle clips. Rainwater is collecting in a pool around my feet. I must look a sight. I remove the mac and fold it over my arms; holding it like a duvet, I stand in front of him. I manage a smile, but he doesn't smile back. I speak instead:

'Hello.'

I couldn't think what else to say. He nods, mute. I wonder whether he *can* speak.

'I was just cycling past, so …' I shrug, trailing off.

Perhaps this wasn't such a good idea. Perhaps I should come back later – with something to offer, something to give: flowers, chocolates, Lucozade.

'Thank you,' he says.

His voice, when it comes, is a shock. I was expecting an agonised croak, but it's startlingly normal, as though he were merely an actor in a hospital drama.

'As I said, I was just passing, so …' I swallow, trying to think what else to say. 'Are you in pain?'

He's half sitting up in bed. The bed, I can't help thinking, is angled back like a car seat in The Classic (one of my favourite positions). There are tubes coming out of him somewhere and going into him somewhere else. But I don't want to stare – to make him feel uncomfortable. In his lap is a book of poetry, closed around his thumb and index finger. Around his right bicep is a padded white bandage, where his tattoo used to be. The thought of the raw wound beneath sends electric currents down the backs of my legs.

'No,' he says. 'Morphine. Lots of it.'

That explains the heavy eyelids.

'Lucky you,' I reply, immediately wishing I hadn't.

For a while, we don't speak. I walk to the wall-sized window and look out. Or, rather, down. The town below is ragged, drained of colour, like an over-washed fabric. The view is hazy with a mist of rain. I can hear the electric bleep of his heart monitor. I think, just like in films: *the hospital scene*.

'I suppose you know about the house,' I say, turning round and leaning against the window; it cools my back through my M&S shirt.

'Yes,' he says.

'What happened?'

'It was last night. Ismael phoned me here. A brick through the window. Petrol through the letterbox. Then the carpet get burned. After they use water for the fire, they go outside and they see the writing.'

Ismael is the Angolan refugee who lives in the house.

'Was anybody hurt?'

'No. But Makhmut was shocked. He was sleep in the living room. He had glass in his hair from the window.'

Makhmut is the Chechen.

'And the attack, in the town centre, who were they?'

Tariq turns away from me and looks towards the empty corridor. He blinks, his curly-lashed eyes filmy. Next to the white sheets his skin looks dark, the colour of wet sand.

'I don't know. But it was a plan. They knew me.'

'How?'

'They see the photos.'

'What photos?'

'The photos.' He turns to me, his head against the pillow. 'Of me. Of Lucy P. In the car. Remember?'

Synaptic lightning. Of course – they saw him with Lucy P

on the website. FUCK OUR WOMEN AND WE FUCK YOU. Could they have identified him from his tattoo? I lean back, resting my head against the glass.

'Jesus.'

Again, we're silent. There are voices echoing down the corridor, but I can't tell from which direction.

'By the way,' I say, still blinking at the ceiling. 'How do you *know* Lucy P?'

When he doesn't answer, I lower my gaze.

'You introduced me to her,' he says.

'Did I? When?'

'A few weeks ago. At work.'

'At *work*?'

'Yes.' Suddenly, he's almost smiling. 'When I repair your computer one time, I saw some message from her. You were in the kitchen, making tea. She seem like an interesting lady, so I wrote down her e-mail.' He holds up his palm feebly. 'I'm sorry.'

I laugh briefly. 'Christ, don't be. I just wondered, that's all. I haven't heard her complaining.'

I look out of the window again. This time, I notice a second car park at the back of the hospital, shrunken by aerial distance: a charcoal duvet, stitched with neat white boxes. It's hemmed in by trees on three sides. Interesting.

'So when can I come back for work?' asks Tariq.

I turn to him and shrug. 'I don't know. When you feel like it. There's no hurry. You need time to recover.'

'I am bored here, in this bed.' He looks around the room, before returning his eyes to me: black, moist, angry. His mood has darkened. 'I want to go to work, to my car, to my *life*. This is not life here, in this hospital.'

'Why don't you ask the doctor? See what he thinks.'

'She,' says Tariq. 'The doctor is a woman.'

'Oh,' I reply, limply.

We fall to silence once more. The hypnotic pulse of his

heart monitor reminds me of the early video games of my childhood. I remember the tennis game that consisted of nothing more than two white lines and a white dot. *Blip. Blip.* Back and forth. Back and forth.

'Is there anyone in other countries you want me to contact?' I ask, uncertainly. 'You know – friends, acquaintances, extended family.'

Tariq doesn't answer; I wonder if he heard me.

'I mean, I don't mind writing letters or making phone calls. Although language might—'

'There is no one,' he interrupts.

I nod. 'Right.'

From the corridor, I hear footsteps; they clack with the sound of hard high heels. A white-coated doctor enters – slim, black haired, possibly Middle Eastern. She glances at me, smiles brittlely, then turns her attention immediately to Tariq. I decide to make myself scarce. On my way out, I pass Tariq's bed:

'See you soon.'

He nods at me, heavy eyed, as the doctor tends to his bandaged arm. Standing in the lift, as the metal doors close, I hear them speaking in what sounds like Arabic.

4

WE'RE IN A MUSTY THIRD-FLOOR room with large plate-glass windows. The wind brings hailstones against the glass with a sound like ball bearings hitting sheet metal. There are cups on the table and plates of biscuits. My teeth feel furry from coffee and digestives.

We're in an IT meeting, the purpose of which is to decide (after three similar meetings in the past six months) whether or not we should buy an upgraded version of our current program, or invest in a new program entirely. My boss, Tony, is making a case for the latter. He's speaking to the people around the table, marker pen in hand, pointing to things he's drawn on a flip chart. He's stuttery, trembly, red cheeked, impassioned. At first, I assume it's because he's a social cripple who finds public speaking excruciating. But then I realise it's because he actually *cares* which software package we use – he actually *gives* a shit: a realisation that fills me with a macabre, disbelieving fascination. I watch him as I might watch an exotic zoo animal, chowing down on something unspeakable.

Anyway, why he's pouring his heart into this presentation escapes me – we all know that what he's advocating is the more expensive option, and therefore doomed to failure. What's cheapest always wins. I see his failure already in the hooded eyes of the men from the accounts department. Accountants are the most influential people in any organisation – and they know it. That's why they're so unassuming: it's the effortless assurance of power.

From the indistinct wash of voices, a question crystallises in my ears. I glance around; everyone is looking at me. The question is repeated:

'So what do you think, Jeremy?'

I have to pretend I know what they're talking about. I nod slowly and lean forward in my chair. With my elbows on the table, I make a pyramid of my palms. I sigh deeply.

'Well, on balance, I'd have to say I agree with Tony.'

There are fidgets and whispers. I look at Tony, who's standing beside the flip chart, arms hanging limp at his sides. He meets my eyes, crumple chinned, as though I'd just agreed to donate him a kidney. He blinks at me as if to say: *thanks, man*. I nod at him once, and reach for another digestive.

Minutes later, without a single decision having been made, the meeting is adjourned. With our diaries on the table, we agree to have another meeting in two months' time, which will resolve nothing.

I return to my desk and check my voicemail. I lean back in my chair, phone in hand, looking around the strip-lit office. Tariq's desk has remained empty; he's still in hospital, though he's no longer in intensive care. Beside his monitor is a framed photo of his wife and daughter, both murdered in his home country.

The first two messages are internal. The third, to my dismay, is from Marlon. It's the first time he's ever phoned me at work:

> Shep, it's me. I tried your mobile, but it went straight into voicemail. Listen, I need to talk to you. I'm in the shit, man. Give me a bell when you get this. Nice one.

I delete the message and hang up. I slip from the office, descend two flights of stairs and step out into a courtyard that serves as a smoking area. It's deserted. I squint up at the sky: the hail has gone as suddenly as it came, the cloud cut away by lacerating sunlight.

I take my phone from my inside pocket: one missed call. I realise I'd switched it off for the meeting. I glance around, then call Marlon's mobile. As it rings, I walk in circles over the paving slabs; they're strewn with melting hailstones and squashed cigarette butts. Through three wire fences and across a wasteland, I see the back of a secondary school. A girl and a boy, both in uniform, are smoking behind a giant metal bin. They look about fourteen.

'Shep.'

I stop pacing. 'Marlon. I got your message. What's up?'

He sighs gravely. 'Hang on a minute.' I hear the muffled sound of movement and a door being closed. His voice returns, clearer: 'Sorry to phone you at work, blood, but I'm fucking bricking it.'

'Why? What's happened?'

'You remember that couple? The ones we met at the picnic spot on Saturday night?'

'Your friends – Venetia and Simon.'

'Yeah, well, they're not my friends, are they? That's only the third time we've ever met. I barely know them.'

'Oh. So who are they then?'

'*Journalists*. Or he is. Undercover. Acting on a tip-off.'

'*What?* Are you sure? How do you know?'

But already, instinctively, I know that it's true. In retrospect, there were plenty of warning signs: they both asked too many questions, however innocent; and the man was just a *little* too interested in whether or not I was a footballer. He was the hack, she was the bait. Looking back, it was all so obvious. Looking back, it always is.

'Because they're blackmailing me,' he says.

'How?'

The schoolgirl has dropped to her knees.

'They've got the film.'

'What film?'

'The film you shot – on the video camera. Of me and Bianca.'

'But I thought that camera was yours?'

'It was theirs. They brought it with them, and I was dumb enough to use it, wasn't I?'

'But hang on – I'm in that film too. You filmed me shagging Bianca on the bonnet.'

The schoolboy is unzipping his flies.

'Yeah, but you're not famous, are you? You're not even *married*. How are they going to blackmail you? Threaten to tell your parents?'

'But they're in that video themselves – Venetia and Simon. I filmed them fucking in the back of their jeep.'

'*Did* you, though? Are you sure that's what they were doing? Or did it just *look* like that's what they were doing? How d'you know they didn't fake the whole thing?'

'Good point,' I say, reasonably. 'I was pretty distracted. By Bianca, mostly.'

'Anyway, it doesn't matter now. It's their camera, their video – they can do what they like with it.'

The boy is gripping the girl's hair.

'So what are they saying?' I ask. 'What do they want?'

'What d'you think they want? – Money.'

'How much?'

He tells me: it's the size of an average mortgage.

'Or what? What if you don't cough up?'

'They'll put the film on the internet. They've already bought a site for it, they reckon. And then they'll sell the story to a tabloid.'

The back of the girl's head is moving.

'Jesus. That means that *I'd* be on the internet too.'

'I doubt it, guy. They'd probably edit you out. I mean, no offence, but who'd want to watch you? I'm the main attraction, aren't I?'

'True.' I don't know whether to feel relieved or crestfallen.

'So what should I do?'

I shake my head despairingly. 'I don't know. What do you reckon?'

'Well – pay the bastards. If this gets out, I'm *fucked*, big time. Stacy will leave me, and I'll lose all my contracts. I'd have to try and make another record.'

I'm mentally spoilt for sardonic responses. But I manage to say:

'But how d'you know they won't take your money and do it anyway? They'd make a killing if they sold that film online.'

'Because then I'd tell everyone what they'd done – that they'd blackmailed me, and that they're a couple of fucking scumbags.'

'But who would listen? Your name would be dirt by then. And who would care? Everyone'd be too busy downloading the video, wouldn't they?'

The schoolgirl rises to her feet.

'*Fuck!*' says Marlon, after a long silence. 'Fucking ... *cunts!*'

'Perhaps you should play for time?' I suggest, trying to calm him down. 'Sound them out. Maybe negotiate. Even meet up with them. At least you'd get an idea of who you're dealing with – what kind of people they are.'

'I suppose.' Marlon sighs, wearily. 'I just can't believe I fell for it, you know? I can't believe I was so fucking ... *stupid*.'

I shrug sympathetically. 'But how were you to know? It was a sting – a set-up. It could've happened to anybody.'

The boy is tugging the girl's knickers down her thighs.

'But it didn't, did it? It happened to Yours Truly ... Hang on a sec.' I hear him speak away from the phone, hand over the receiver. His voice comes back, quieter: 'Listen, something's come up, I've got to go. Speak to you later, yeah?'

'All right,' I say. 'Keep me posted.'

I put my phone away and head for the building. Before I enter, I look back towards the school: the boy is on his knees with his head under the girl's skirt. The girl has a cigarette in one hand and a mobile phone in the other. She's angling it above her swaying crotch, filming the boy in action.

5

THAT EVENING, out of pure curiosity, I log on to YouTube. I search for a clip of a schoolboy going down on a schoolgirl. I can't find one. Perhaps it was never posted in the first place. Or maybe it's been removed already – replaced, as usual, by that spoilsport euphemism: USER VIOLATION.

I log off YouTube and go to Google. I type in Marlon's celebrity name and 'sex video'. After 0.43 seconds, I have a list of websites. All are typographical flukes – except the first. I click on the link. The page that appears is blank except for a single line in the top-left corner: UNDER CONSTRUCTION. Christ, these people are serious. I toy with the idea of phoning Marlon to tell him, then decide against it: he's rattled enough as it is.

Instead, I go to Hotmail to check for messages. In my inbox, sandwiched between several layers of spam – *Herbal Viagra, Are You Lonely?, Young And Horny, Slack Granny* – is an e-mail from Lucy P:

From: lucy_p@rocketmail.com
To: shep69@hotmail.com
Subject: Tariq

Shep,

I take it you've heard about Tariq. Couldn't believe it – absolutely terrible. i might go and visit him in hospital. Is it safe d'you think?

btw – what are you doing Friday pm? Want to meet up?

Lucy P xxx

I tap off a reply:

From: shep69@hotmail.com
To: lucy_p@rocketmail.com
Subject: Re: Tariq

Darling Lucy P,

Yes, I did hear about Tariq. I went to see him myself. Pop your head round – I'm sure he'd appreciate it. There's no danger.

Friday evening would be great. Let's speak nearer the time.

The Shep xxx

I click 'Send' and lean back in my chair. Through the open window, I hear the low judder of a police helicopter.

6

I'M CYCLING ALONG suburban streets, whirring over tarmac through orange cones of street light. The night-time air is warm, thin and moistureless. According to weather reports, it's already the hottest May since records began. Every year, it seems, it's the hottest, coldest, wettest, driest, rainiest, sunniest, snowiest, humidest, whatever-est year since records began. I can't enjoy the weather any more, even when it's fine: it feels mutant, schizophrenic. A world has been lost; dumbly, over our steering wheels, we watched it depart. The generation that did nothing: that's how they'll remember us.

Through air buffing my ears, I hear a beeping sound from my kitbag. Wondering if it's Lucy P, whom I'm on my way to meet – and dreading a last-minute hitch – I stop in the gutter to take out my mobile. With a tingle of relief in my penis, I see that the message is from Marlon. In the darkness, the screen is translucent, an illuminated square of ice:

> Shep, met up with those 2 journos. surprisingly
> reasnable. wanted to fuckin pummel them
> but just paid up instead. Everything cool now.
> sory you wont be famous porn * on internet

I replace the phone in my bag – it nestles between a ripe banana and a tube of lubricant – and resume my pedalling.

My journey, I realise, will take me past a popular pub in

my town: the Rose and Crown. It's a chain pub, vaguely Irish themed – you know this from the half-hearted green paintwork and the odd picture of a shamrock – with a rainbow of bottles in neon-lit refrigerators, quiz and fruit machines playing maddening jingles, and dispensers in the toilets selling fruit-flavoured condoms.

It used to have a reputation for underage drinking; for a generation of local teenagers, it was the only place to get pissed. One of the reasons is that it's tucked away here, in this bland residential suburb, a couple of miles from the pub-packed town centre. Most of the houses contain families, which means a guaranteed supply of hard-drinking teenagers. Many of these teenagers will soon have babies of their own (from drunken encounters), thereby establishing the next generation (of hard-drinking teenagers). It's no surprise – there's little else to do in my town except have babies. And shop. And fight. And fuck.

But when new management took it over, the Rose and Crown targeted a different crowd – people in their twenties with a bit of money, drawn mainly from the business park down the road: accountants, solicitors, surveyors, estate agents. It's now a hot spot for after-work drinks and chintzy office parties.

Swinging on to a double-parked road, my wheels *tick-ticking* as I glide without pedalling, the night-warm air blowing over my face, I can hear the pub already. I remember that it's Friday night. I check my watch: 11.19 p.m. I catch some music – hey, something by Marlon's old band! – wavering in volume as the pub's double doors open and shut. Other sounds drift towards me on the darkness. Laughter. Male shouts. Female screams. Glass splintering. Car engines revving. Somebody being sick. The single *whurrrp!* of a police car or ambulance. Gliding around a corner, on to the same road as the pub, I'm met with a scene reminiscent of the aftermath of a terrorist attack. People are passing through the pub's double doors, jostled by bouncers wearing black leather jackets and radio earpieces. On a grass verge, a woman in a silver sequin dress and a pink Afro wig is on all fours, puking into a gutter. Another woman, wearing exactly the same outfit, staggers towards her, pint glass in hand. She sits on her friend's naked back; the puking woman collapses on to her belly. The beer sloshes out of her glass on to her friend's head. Both of them burst into high-pitched giggles. A young man wearing a DKNY top and no helmet pulls away from the pub on a Honda moped, chased by two others. One of them, who is wearing a pinstriped suit, yells 'Fucking prick!' and throws a Michelob bottle after him. It smashes in front of me; I swerve to avoid it. Just outside the pub's doors, two men are jabbering at a knife-proof-vested policeman, who is taking notes in a black book with a referee's head-dipped patience. A nearby ambulance slashes them all with blue light. A man is sitting on the back step of the ambulance, eyes closed, head angled upwards. He has blood all over his face and down his shirt and tie; a paramedic is picking glass from his wonky nose. Next to the ambulance is a BMW with its windows wound down. Club music is pumping out; I feel the bass going through my handlebars. Two women are dancing on the bonnet, barefoot, both holding cocktail glasses. One of them spots me looking at them as I pass. She *whoops!*, turns round and lifts her short black dress to reveal a chubby white bottom, peach-halved by a G-string. A red rose is tattooed on her right buttock. I wobble and almost veer into a lamp-post (which earns me a bonus *whoop!*). After I turn another corner, the pub recedes into the night. A white police van passes in the opposite direction; a German Shepherd is barking in the back, the sound Dopplered. Within seconds, I'm alone again – with my bike, my thoughts, my plans, my kitbag.

I cycle on, enjoying the hushed, hair-blown freedom that only cycling can bring. I pass a brand-new housing estate. There's a row of flags at the gated entrance; the flags hang limp in the windless night. Next to the flags is an advertising board that hasn't been taken down yet. That's because not all the flats have been sold. There's a giant banner across the board saying so: 'ONE AND TWO BEDROOM UNITS STILL AVAILABLE!' I wonder what the difference between a 'flat' and a 'unit' is. Space, probably. Or the lack of it. There's probably an arcane legal distinction that prevents them using the word 'flat', so they have to settle for the clinical-sounding 'unit' instead. Everything is studied and calculated. The smallest details conceal design, intelligence. Nothing is an accident. I look at the red-brick blocks as I pass. Out of what must be fifty 'units', there are lights on in just a handful.

That's because they're too expensive. I remember reading an article about them in the local paper, the *F—— Argus*, before they were built. Originally, they were intended for key workers: carers, nurses, firemen, teachers – people doing self-less jobs for peanuts. But the prices weren't realistic. I enquired about them myself (out of curiosity more than intention). A one-bedroom place would have stretched the salary of a single lawyer, let alone a single nurse. So these carpet-smelling 'units' remain uninhabited. *Nobody* in my town can afford them. The empty kennels await their dogs.

The town is running out now. Street lights are dying. Parked cars are thinning at kerbsides. Houses are morphing into trees and hedges.

The smell is changing too. The flavours of dew-freshened grass and blossoming flowers are being pushed out by heavier, richer, sourer smells that stick to the back of the throat – sweat-soaked fur, ground-down hoofs, liquid dung, a thou-sand buckets of blood. I look to my right: I see a perimeter fence topped with razor wire so perfectly spiralled that it looks almost decorative; a Checkpoint Charlie whose twin glass booths are weakly illuminated by flickering grey monitors; CCTV cameras on high metal poles at thirty-metre intervals; and a low, featureless, colourless building whose surfaces are lit by greasy yellow floodlights. The only distinctive detail is a squat metal chimney, shaped like the letter 'Y'.

The smell is at its strongest now, condensing at the back of my throat – it drips in a mercurial thread to form a tepid pool of nausea in my stomach. On a rare swirl of wind, the low-pitched groans of cattle reach me from the building. A machine whirrs with electric efficiency, metallic-sounding. I speed up my pedalling; the smell fades away, diluted by the smells of the passing foliage. As the building slips behind me, it seems to intensify its own silence and the silence of the countryside around it – to suck all sounds towards it, like a black hole in the fabric of the landscape, from which sound, not light, can never escape.

7

I'M ON MY WAY TO A SITE that Lucy P suggested. It's brand new, which means one of two things: either it'll be packed or it'll be deserted. There'll be no halfway house.

Sites have to be changed frequently; it's the only way to stay ahead of the police. Once a site has been discovered, it immediately gets blacklisted – by e-mail, by chatroom, by text message, by word of mouth. Nobody will touch it.

And the community is adaptable, dynamic; like water, it seeks out cracks, spaces, channels. This is a human law: if people want to do something, it's impossible to stop them doing it

Here's my answer – the site is packed. I realise where I am now: at a disused tennis club two miles south of my town. I've passed it several times in cars and buses. It comprises four grass tennis courts, bounded by a high wire fence, and a pavilion-type building, which once served as changing rooms and a café.

But now it's a vision of entropy. As I pass on my bike, my eyes run over it. The fence is rusted and torn in places, leaving large shabby flaps hanging down. The grass courts are sickly khaki and weed-studded. The nets look fragile and ragged, as if they've been nibbled at by giant moths. The white bands at the top of the nets have all turned grey.

Yet out of this nest of stagnation flutter light, movement

and energy. Through gaps in the hedge, I can see white headlights, red brake lights, turning hubcaps, human figures shuffling restlessly.

Only there's little sound. People on the circuit have been conditioned to be quiet. Of all the things that might give you away, noise is the prime culprit. Apart from the odd cough of a car ignition, the gentle crumping of feet over gravel, the site is near-silent. What you rarely hear are human voices. People on the circuit don't do much talking anyway.

I dismount, kill my lights and wheel my bike along the side of the road. Already, after my four-mile cycle ride, I can feel that I'm about to sweat. I stop, reach inside my kitbag and, with my roll-on deodorant, give my armpits a fresh going over under my shirt. Being a little sweaty is forgivable; *smelling* a little sweaty isn't.

Finally, I see a gap in the hedge: the car park's entrance. There's a rusted metal sign coming out of the tarmac:

S—— M—— Lawn Tennis Club

Private members only

24 hour CCTV surveillance

Not once in my life, even when I earned plenty of money in London, have I belonged to a private tennis club. By the looks of it, it's too late to join this one. I lean my bike against the sign and D-lock it to the metal pole.

I walk through the gap, kitbag over my shoulder. I stop to survey the scene. In the smallish gravel car park are nine or ten cars. I recognise the number plates of three of them: all regulars. Most of the punters who are on foot (eight or nine at a glance) are gathered around a single car – a dark Volvo estate. That must be where the show is. Generally, at these meets, the sex passes from car to car, like a baton; it tends not to happen in several cars simultaneously. This is to get the greatest voyeuristic – and, for the couples, exhibitionistic – mileage out of the gathering. When the Volvo couple have finished, another couple in another car will get started. And the punters who are still interested will shuffle towards it, bumping into one another silently, like cattle.

I scan the site from a security viewpoint: it isn't ideal. Over the years, I've come to develop an instinct for sites – and this one feels vulnerable. There are no surveillance cameras (probably removed long ago), but nor is there an enclosed area for the shows: no 'pen' of trees or hedges to offer cover from all directions. Instead, there's only the derelict pavilion building and the broken hedge – which, together, form an elongated 'L' shape – to separate the site from the road.

Still, what it does have in its favour is remoteness. It's a good few miles from the town centre and beyond the edge of the suburbs. There are unlikely to be any casual passers-by. Everyone who comes here will know what they've come here for.

I hear a car behind me. I turn to see a grey Mini, head-lights off, pulling into the car park. I step aside to let it cruise past. Its wheels are just centimetres from my toes. It's impossible to see through the tinted glass; I wonder how the driver can see out.

The question is, where's Lucy P? Has she even arrived yet? I can't see her among the punters, although it's too dark to be sure of people's faces. Besides, judging by their arm movements, all the punters are men. This means that she might be in one of the cars. But which one?

Tentatively, on foot, I begin a slow circuit of the car park. I squint into windscreens from a distance of a few metres. Many of the cars are empty; others contain the outlines of figures. In two or three, I see couples illuminated by interior lights. The lights go out as soon as I approach them. They think I'm looking for a show and are signalling that they're not ready.

I come to the scrum of men around the Volvo. I try to find a place to stand, but it's not easy. One of the circuit's cardinal sins is to block somebody else's view. This can make positioning tricky. I shuffle from spot to spot, checking over my shoulder to ensure I'm in nobody's eyeline – like somebody edging around a packed-out pub, searching for a spot from which to watch the football. Eventually, I find a poor location at the front of the car (the prime spots to the side and rear have all been taken). Given that the couple are lying in the back with the seats folded down, I've ended up viewing them over the bonnet and dashboard: the worst seat in the house.

Still, they're going at it enthusiastically. They're doing it missionary style, which is all the space allows. I can just about make them out from where I'm standing (hands at my sides, kitbag over my shoulder, anonymous among the silent punters). Neither of them is an oil painting. Both are in their late forties, at a guess, with average-to-uglyish faces. The man has a greasy comb-over; the woman's hair is a bird's nest. Their bodies are pale, flabby and shapeless; they sweat, grunt and fumble. This is the reality of human intercourse – and it's glorious. If I'd wanted a bleach-teethed fantasy, or silicon-honed perfection, I'd have stayed at home and watched pornography. Many regard pornography as a corruption of sex. On the contrary: sex is a corruption of pornography. Pornography is a dream of human sex, purified of human reality.

Here, on the circuit, it's a dream from which we've awoken. We've rejected pornographic fantasy in favour of sexual realism. Watching the couple in the car, I'm reminded of Dennis Potter's *Cold Lazarus* (1994), set in a dystopian future England, in which virtual-reality technology has become so sophisticated that it's impossible to distinguish what's real from what's fabricated. A terrorist organisation, Reality Or Nothing (R.O.N.), sabotages this technology, believing it to be an affront to human dignity.

Although our cause isn't as noble as theirs, nor as self-conscious, we too are involved in a kind of struggle. Our unspoken enemy, for want of a more elegant word, is *pornographication* – of human sex, and of culture in general. What we do here is neither an extension of pornography, nor its adjunct. Rather, it's retaliation – against pornography's artifice, its illusion. We're early ancestors of the R.O.N. movement: an underground network of reality terrorists.

There, in the Volvo, is one of our cells. I tip my head to one side, looking at them. Despite their unappealing bodies, they *are* beautiful. But it's the beauty of vulnerability, of perishability. You'll find it in Lucian Freud paintings – a beauty predicated on human frailty. In fact, they look like a couple of Freud nudes, magically come to life: rumpled clothes, untoned limbs, lined faces, greying flesh. No piercings, no bottle tan, no silicon, no make-up. All human.

And putting on the best show they can. Exhibitionism is popularly associated with egotism, but I've always associated it with selflessness: it's primarily a giving. The same accusation is often levelled at the artistic impulse – that it's driven by vanity, narcissism, *Wille zur Macht* – but what really drives it is generosity, an overflowing of spirit. Looked at this way, the couple in front of me are a pair of performance artists. And judging by the flexing elbows around me, they've found an appreciative audience.

I hear a telltale croak to my side, to which I don't pay much attention. I pay more attention when I feel a warm spatter hit my hand. I'm about to turn to my neighbour to thank him, sarcastically, for jizzing on me, when I feel a tap on my shoulder: it's Lucy P, standing beside me in a hooded top. She's pulled the hood over her head, like a hijab.

'Oh, fuck, it's you,' I whisper.

'Thanks a lot.'

'Where did you spring from?'

'I've just got here.'

'How?'

With her head, she gestures towards the pavilion: I see a

light Mercedes parked in front of it. Whether or not it's hers, I don't ask. It may belong to her latest boyfriend, who's mingled with the punters. Then again, it may not. With Lucy P, you never know.

'So what do you think of this place?' she whispers.

I cock a shoulder. 'Not bad. I've seen better. How did you find it?'

'On the web. It's pretty new. I'd heard it was popular.'

'For now,' I reply.

'For now,' she echoes.

'I thought it was just going to be the two of us?' I say, jauntily, to hide my disappointment. 'A cosy little tête-à-tête.'

'The more the merrier, I thought.'

Deflated, I turn my attention back to the car. The middle-aged couple are still going at it. They ought to wrap it up soon; people are growing impatient. Restlessness, like a rumour, is spreading through the crowd. More DNA, I sense, is about to fly through the night.

'Did you go and see Tariq?'

She nods. 'I did. He seemed very down – understandably. Maybe he'll feel better now he's been discharged. Is he back at work yet?'

'No. He's on compassionate leave. But he should be back within a week.'

'D'you think he'll give it up?'

I frown. 'Give what up?'

'Well, you know, this – the scene.'

I shrug. 'Too early to tell. I doubt it. But I wouldn't blame him if he did.'

'Who were they? The people who attacked him.'

'No idea. They could have been anybody. There were no witnesses – apparently. Have you heard about Marlon?'

No sooner have I said this than I wish I hadn't. I shouldn't mention what happened with the journalists. If Marlon wants to tell Lucy P, he'll do so when he's good and ready.

'No? What?'

I have to think on my feet: 'He's just secured some new TV work. He says it pays an absolute fortune. He's over the moon about it.'

'Wow!' She seems to buy it. 'Good for him. I'll have to text him to say congratulations.'

'Nah!' I whisper. 'You needn't bother. He said it's no big deal.'

'Oh. But you just said—'

I nudge her with my elbow and nod towards the Volvo. 'Here we go.'

Lucy P arches on her tiptoes to get a better view. To steady herself, she rests her fingertips on my shoulder. Volts of arousal tingle through my nerve endings. Some people just have that effect on you. Together, we watch – balanced, like statuettes. The man in the back of the car has reared up on his hands, as if he's halfway through a press-up. Judging by his expression (as though he's about to explode into tears), we all know what's going to happen next.

'I give him five seconds,' I say.

'Three,' whispers Lucy P, her breath warm on my earlobe.

Then, without warning, as if somebody has just let off tear gas, the punters scatter. The man in the Volvo rolls off the woman and scrambles in the car for his trousers. I look around, bewildered. And then I see: a police car is coming towards us, blue lights spinning. I turn round to warn Lucy P, but she's already vanished. Without breaking into a run, which would only make me more conspicuous, I avert my face and walk swiftly towards the exit. But just as I reach it, I see another police car blocking the way. Clever: send one car in to flush us out; keep another car back to lie in wait. In an instant decision, I dart sideways, blue light flickering my face, and head for the pavilion. There, at the far end, away from the police car, I find a pile of tables, stacked four or five high, with a padlocked chain around their legs. I step over the padlock –

it clinks rustily after I clip it with my heel; I wince – and squat under the tables. The air smells of rotting wood and damp soil. A cobweb sticks to my face like candyfloss. In summers past, I imagine, people sat at these tables in tennis whites, sipping Pimms and discussing line calls. Where are all those people now? Perhaps they're here, scattered through the night, using the club for its contemporary purpose.

As I squat in the dark, my heart pounds a dent in my chest. After several years on the circuit, this is my first real brush with the police. I've always sensed their presence at the edge of things – like a heat, like a light – but I've yet to get burnt. Until now, they'd never got close enough.

But why tonight? The site struck me as exposed from the outset, but I can't believe two squad cars just happened to be passing. Someone must have told them we were coming. Someone must have given them a tip-off.

From under the tables, I peer over at the Volvo. The scene is illuminated by flashing blue lights. Every few seconds, I hear the *crhcrhcrch!* of the squad car's radio. I can't help being impressed by the police – by their uniforms, their equipment, their seriousness. A young policewoman is questioning the couple who were having sex. She makes notes while the man and woman adjust their hair and clothes, nodding and answering politely. There isn't a hint of malice or protest; they merely look contrite, like a couple of teenagers caught out by their parents. All perfectly English. I wonder what the police will do with them. Will they get off with a warning? Will they be charged with 'indecency' or 'lewdness'? (What's the difference?) Can they be charged with anything at all?

The car park is deserted now. Everyone has vanished, including Lucy P. Or that's what it looks like. In reality, most of the punters are probably still around, lurking behind whatever they could find: cars, trees, hedges, bushes. I can't believe I'm the only one left, sweating in the dark. Besides, there are still nine or ten cars in the car park; not one of them escaped.

The other police officer – tall, young, burly, square shouldered – is walking from car to car. I watch his procedure, which he repeats meticulously. With his torch, he checks each interior. Then he steps back, holds a digital camera at arm's length and takes a picture of the car (which I presume includes its number plate). Each time, the camera punches the night with a fist of colour, before the darkness heals over again. Psychedelic blobs are floating across my retinae.

And now he's heading my way. Sweat dampens my palms. I see the powerful beam of his police torch moving in quick, dazzling, light-trailed zigzags. He's inspecting the pavilion, from the opposite end. I hear a rustling sound from a bush near by: two figures scamper across the grass, backs hunched, as if they're running under helicopter blades. The policeman is getting closer to me. From under the tables, I see his legs from the knees down. His torch scours the building greedily – an airborne creature on a lead of white light, sniffing out life. He's about ten metres away (now nine, now eight). I feel weirdly divided: a part of me is terrified, like a fox being hunted down; but another part of me is fearless, even defiant. I have a short-lived urge to spring up and confront him. *Here I am!* I want to shout. *What are you going to do about it? Arrest me for squatting under a table?*

I don't, of course. Instead, I shrink to the back of the table as his booted feet approach. I tuck my chin into my chest to conceal my face. I hold my black kitbag over my head for camouflage. The torch illuminates the underside of the table in a brilliant flash. The boots squelch in the mud, a metre from where I'm squatting. I hear his breathing, interrupted by the *crhcrhcrh!* of his police radio, deafening up so close. Then his footsteps recede across the earth. I lower my bag and look up. The policeman has joined his female colleague, who's still talking to the Volvo couple. They've straightened out their clothes and look entirely respectable – like a couple of teachers or magistrates, out walking their poodles.

I stay where I am, watching. Nothing much is happening. The police and the couple are chatting amiably. I take this opportunity to get in some meditation. I close my eyes to the darkness. Like a bat, I attempt to use sound to visualise my surroundings, to create a sonic map. I listen to the wind in the leaves, trying to picture each one – trying to match each mental leaf with its real-life rustle.

But just as I begin to feel calm, an engine disturbs my concentration. My eyes blink open. The police car is driving off; their work here is done. They know that people won't re-emerge in their presence (they have photos, anyway, of their cars and number plates). Then the couple drive off too, their Volvo crackling the gravel. The curtain has fallen on their stymied performance.

Moments follow of stillness and quiet. I'm careful not to move. The wind fingers the leaves. Something squeaks on a hinge. I look out at the world from under the tables. On the horizon, the sky is grainy blue; a meteorite sparks its powdery surface.

From somewhere, an owl *hoo-hoos*. It seems to act like an air-raid siren, announcing the all-clear. People start emerging from trees and hedges. Behind me, I hear a scraping sound – I flinch in shock, hitting my head on the roof of the table. Insects and debris patter my shoulders. All along, I realise, someone was crouching beside me. I watch a lone figure walk off towards the car park.

As people leave their hiding places, the site comes back to life. But only briefly – nobody's hanging about. Car doors clunk shut. Engines fire and rev. Headlights ignite the darkness. Game over. There's nothing stopping me leaving either; I ought to head off. But I don't – I stay in my hiding place, muscles frozen.

Ten minutes later, when the site is deserted, I come out. I walk over the grass towards the car park. The dew is sinking into my Hush Puppies; its wetness is prickling my toes. I reach the spot where the Volvo was parked. I feel listless, dreamy, melancholic. I'm the only person left. In fact, I'm probably the only person for miles. I look up at the darkened sky – at its ancient light, its star-stretched emptiness. Never has the idea of God felt more absurd.

Then I realise what I'm waiting for. Or, rather, whom: Lucy P. I'd hoped that she'd be waiting for me too; that she'd reappear for unfinished business. But there's no sign of her – the light Mercedes has vanished. With head-in-the-sand hope, I decide to wait five minutes.

There's nothing to do. I scuff around the car park, eating the banana from my kitbag. I notice some debris at my feet: a soiled tissue, some tangled Y-fronts, a coil of orange peel and a condom packet. Then I spot a white card, lying face down. I pick it up and flip it over:

The Shep

shep69@hotmail.com
07977 218 638

Safety, pleasure, discretion

It's one of my contact cards, the kind I give out on the circuit. But where did it come from? Did it fall out of my pocket? Did Lucy P bring it with her? Or are there more in circulation than I thought? I stand there, chewing my banana, glassy eyed, wondering if that's good or bad.

I look at my watch: the five minutes are up. With a cool heart, I check my phone for messages: nothing. I put all the litter in a carrier bag and head for the exit.

I approach my bike, still D-locked to the sign (my heart

warms: it's always a relief to see that your bike hasn't been nicked). But as I near it, I slow down. I walk around it in a fascinated arc – as though I'm approaching an exhibit in an art gallery. It looks wrecked. The wheels have been buckled, their spokes sticking out like antennae. The chain has been snapped and hangs, limp, from the rear wheel's sprockets. The brake cables have been cut and are as frayed as raw spaghetti. It's a mountain bike as Dali might imagine it – melted, beaten-up.

I spot something on the saddle and step forward. Over the black leather, in what looks like white paint, is a single word:

PERVERT

I run my fingertips over the letters, but they're too dry to smudge.

In my peripheral vision, I detect light. I turn to see a car coming towards me. I dart behind the metal sign, crouch down and peer over my knackered bike. It's a police car, cruising through the darkness. As it passes, my eyes run over its waxy surface. In the front are the two young officers. In the back, at the window, is Lucy P, her face tear-glistened.

8

ON MONDAY MORNING, now my bike is out of action, my mother gives me a lift to work. I feel like a ten-year-old, sitting beside her in the passenger seat. I wish I'd walked. The traffic is barely moving. It seems to be made up entirely of parents taking fat children to school in 4x4s. Over the white noise of the car radio, I hear the windscreen wipers. *Clunk squeak clunk. Clunk squeak clunk.*

I look out of the drizzled window. On the deserted pavement, brake lights tremble in acidic puddles. Beyond the pavement, set back from the road, are out-of-town superstores. Each one is the size of an aircraft hangar. Through leaves and branches, swaying silently through the glass, I spot the telltale blue-yellow of the new IKEA. Someone was stabbed to death in the stampede on the day it opened. Such is the world's passion for flat-packed Swedish furniture. There's no knowing what will catch on, is there? – no knowing *what* people will go for (which is presumably why Ernö Rubrik never got his cube patented). According to newspapers, the murder weapon was a metal rod that formed part of a scented candlestick holder. Before I get out, I catch a fragment of a news report:

> —issued through his solicitor said that he regretted the incident and was deeply sorry for the pain and embarrassment it had caused his—

My mother distracts me: 'Will you be home for dinner tonight?'

Whether or not I'm home for dinner is a very big deal to my parents. I sometimes wonder if they plan their whole day around it. The older they get, the more they like to organise – the less they like *anything* to be spontaneous. I live under their roof, so naturally I go with it.

'Yes.' They also prefer clear, concise, unambiguous answers. My hand is already on the door release. 'Definitely.'

'What d'you fancy? You can have pasta shells in cheese sauce or vegetable lasagne.'

It's 8.13 in the morning: how can she know what the choice is?

'Lasagne, please.'

My mother nods, satisfied, as if she suspected I'd plump for lasagne. There's nothing she likes better than having her intuitions confirmed. 'And I'll buy some of that raspberry ice cream,' she adds, snapping the indicator stick and checking her wing mirror. 'The one you like.'

'Thanks, Mum.'

I watch her yellow Peugeot slip back into the traffic. The cars form a sluggish, unending queue into the rain-smudged distance. Traffic, everywhere, is getting slower – from provincial England to metropolitan China. You don't have to be a driver to notice it. If you plotted the average global traffic speed (y-axis) against time in years (x-axis), the line would slope downwards, left to right, like an *accent grave*. It would then be possible to estimate the point at which the line touches the x-axis. This would tell you, theoretically, when the average traffic speed on Earth will reach zero: the moment of absolute global gridlock.

I turn from the road to face the perimeter fence around my building. The building, like so many in my town, is a sixties monstrosity. But even if I worked in a Florentine church, I still wouldn't feel like going in today. There's no particular reason – I just can't be fucked. I wonder if, on some days, everybody feels like this, irrespective of status. Do presidents sometimes think, *I can't be arsed to run my country today*? Do heads of state phone in sick? For a moment, I contemplate doing exactly that – or getting back into my mother's car, which has only moved about five metres.

Instead, I stare up at one of the CCTV cameras: it stares back at me, like a giant snail's eye. Shit. I might have been seen now; I can't just bunk off. I remain on the pavement, motionless. Over my sleepy face, rain is pulsing in gentle layers. I feel like meditating, right here, right now, but there's too much traffic – I don't want to look like a lunatic in front of all those drivers. Holding my supermarket carrier bag, which contains a novel, an apple and two Marmite sandwiches, I drag myself towards the Checkpoint Charlie.

The geezer who sits in the glass box on the left is called Keith. The geezer who sits in the glass box on the right is called Barry. Normally, they're pretty vigilant, keeping an eye on all the comings and goings. But today, they're entirely useless. Walking through the checkpoint, I glance up at Barry's booth: they're both crammed in there, hip to hip, ensconced in a tabloid newspaper. Page 3, I reckon. Must be a good one. I pass through the checkpoint completely unchallenged. I could be wearing a turban, combat fatigues and carrying a bazooka.

The office is deserted. I love it when it's like this. There's nothing more tranquil than a deserted office: the sleeping printers, the hibernating computers, the framed photos of dogs and babies, the cups of cold coffee, surfaces still as mirrors. A ruffled silence.

I look over at Tariq's desk – still no Tariq. I hang up my coat, the first on the stand, and sit at my workstation. I start up Windows, which plays a little tune – it sounds louder than usual, amplified by the silence. When I tuck into my e-mail, I see an internal message. It has a little red exclamation mark beside it:

To: All Staff
From: IT Support
Subject: For Your Urgent Attention

Dear All,

Please be reminded that the viewing of websites of an adult nature is strictly prohibited on any computer anywhere on these premises.

Failure to abide by this regulation (4.27: A) could result in serious disciplinary action.

Regards,
IT Support

I can only assume, as my cheeks start to redden, that this message is intended for me. Has somebody, somewhere, taken exception to the sites I've been visiting? Surely not. After all, Gavin, head of IT, is my friend and colleague, so why wouldn't he have warned me?

But, then, perhaps he isn't my friend at all? Maybe I read it all wrong? Perhaps it's all in my head? With some people, you never quite know. Fear spreads through my stomach, like internal bleeding.

I dial his extension; he always gets in early. His office is on the floor above. He'll know it's me because my name and number will appear on his telephone (*Jeremy Shepherd 4452*). I swivel left and right in my chair, jittery, looking across the paper-strewn desks.

'Hi, Jem.'

'Gavin.' My voice booms in the silence. Instinctively, I lower it, even though the office is empty. 'Listen. That e-mail you sent round – I've just read it. I was wondering ... anything I need to know?'

Down the phone, I hear him smile; relief pours through me.

'Don't worry. Purely routine. Merely a reaction to the circumstances.'

'What circumstances?'

'Haven't you seen the papers this morning?'

'No. Why?'

'Have a look. You'll see what I mean.'

Moments later, I head for the table by the water cooler. As usual, the day's newspapers are spread across it, neatly dovetailed. I pick out a high-selling tabloid. On the front page are two colour photographs. One shows Marlon on stage at Wembley Arena at the height of his fame. The other shows the picnic spot in the countryside where I filmed him fucking Bianca. Across the photos is a giant headline:

———'S
PERV-ECT
PICNIC

Ex-boy band star's outdoor sex flick shame

See pages 4 & 5

I lean against the table to stop my legs collapsing. With trembling fingers, I turn the pages:

From front page

—— ——'s life lies in ruins this morning after a shocking **SEX VIDEO** has appeared on the internet.

The amazing video, shot by an anonymous cameraman in a **FAMILY PICNIC SPOT** in ——shire, shows the pervy ex-popster having sex with a gorgeous blonde on the bonnet of a car.

The video, which lasts for nearly **15 MINUTES**, can be downloaded from a fee-paying website.

——'s dirty deed was uncovered by journalist Simon Hogge and ex-model Venetia Carrick who

> lured him to the spot by posing as fellow **SWINGERS** on the internet.
>
> Although —— was unavailable for comment, he issued a statement through his solicitor, apologising to his wife and family.
>
> But it hasn't stopped Radio —— and The —— Channel **TERMINATING** his broadcasting contracts, wrecking his career as a radio DJ and TV presenter.
>
> His gorgeous wife, Music Idol winner Stacy Thompson, fought back her **TEARS** to say, 'I'm totally gutted. I can't believe he's done this to me. I don't know where we go from here.'
>
> The blonde babe who appears in the video is believed to be a **LAP DANCER** from the Birmingham area. Her name and whereabouts are unknown.

With sweat beading my temples, I return to my desk. Already, my thoughts have swerved from Marlon's fate to my own: self-preservation is always the primary instinct.

Which is another way of saying that I'm fixated on the phrase 'anonymous cameraman'. What does that mean? Does it mean that my sex scene with Bianca has been edited out, as Marlon predicted? Or does it mean that it's been left in, and I'm only 'anonymous' in the sense that I haven't yet been identified?

I have a stomach-twisting thought: maybe Gavin was doing me a favour by sending round that e-mail this morning. Perhaps he's seen the video, and has seen that I'm in it, and is desperately trying to protect me.

Panicking, I start up Explorer. I check over my shoulder – all clear – and go to the website. It's no longer 'under construction': it's now a finished product. I see two large stills from the film I shot. One shows Marlon and Bianca smiling into the camera, faces tightly framed. The other shows Bianca on the bonnet of the Jag, about to be taken doggy-style.

There's also a third picture, which shows Marlon with his head inside Bianca's skirt. It's a free ten-second sample clip. I click on it and lean back in my chair. The sound of Bianca's moaning booms out of my computer. I lunge for my mouse to turn the sound off. I glance around self-consciously. I fire the sample up again. Marlon's head starts moving between Bianca's thighs; she's gripping his hair in her amber fingers. I vividly remember filming this sequence.

But it doesn't last long – and it doesn't tell me much. I didn't think it would; it's only a teaser. I close the window and click on a link: 'DOWNLOAD THE FULL-LENGTH VIDEO (14:49 MIN)'. It takes me to a page requesting financial information. The video costs £9.99. With my credit card on my thigh, I type in the relevant details. I start downloading the film on to my desktop.

I wait, nervously drumming my fingers on the mouse. I get up, return to the newspaper table and pick out three tabloids. All of them feature the story on their front pages. There are puns, photos, captions, headlines. I look around and discreetly dump them into a blue recycling bin. I pour some water into a Styrofoam cup; the water cooler farts into its plastic bulb.

Back at my PC, the film has downloaded. It was faster than I thought. I knock back the cold water, sit down, slip on some headphones and click on the video.

The moment it starts, I know that I'm safe. From the very first frame, I'm already behind the camera. Marlon was right, I have been edited out – inevitable, perhaps, in light of my non-celebrity. My prevailing emotion is one of relief; but skulking at its borders is a moody disappointment.

My own safety assured, my thoughts return to Marlon. This will hit his lifestyle hard. He's got more to lose than I have. As I watch, I think again of the couple at the picnic spot: the woman's sticky lips, the man's greasy pate. I feel anger bubbling up in me – burning through my arteries. Violence is never far from life's surface. For a moment, I have a revenge fantasy of travelling back in time, Terminator-style, to deal with them both. Except I wouldn't be carrying my kitbag: I'd be carrying a cricket bat, a metal pipe, a broken bottle, a machete.

Yet nor do I stop watching. Eyes fixed on the screen, my anger mellows into guilty fascination. In the film, I hear Marlon's question as I approach the Jag (*Oi! Blood! Are you still filming or what?*) and my own reply, eerily alien (*Sorry*). Do I really sound like that? So plummy? So nasal? The camera dips and shakes as I stumble on the gravel (*Easy, tiger, easy*). Marlon looks good, and so does Bianca. The film has dulled her orangey suntan, making her look more natural. As they kiss, half-dressed, the camera pans around them smoothly. Not bad – not bad at all. I always suspected I had a flair for cinematography.

Headphones on, I settle back in my chair. I slip my right hand into my trouser pocket. I glance around to make sure that no one else is watching. I spot two of my colleagues, Lee and Jason, on opposite sides of the office. I didn't see them come in. But there's no danger. They're sitting at their PCs too, hands out of sight. Both are wearing headphones, watching their screens intensely.

9

AFTER WORK, HAVING EATEN a vegetable lasagne and raspberry ice cream with my parents, I retire to my room. Sitting on my bed, I call Marlon on my mobile. His phone rings five or six times, then slips into voicemail. I prepare myself to speak, with the lightly sweaty panic that voicemail induces in me:

> Marlon, it's me – The Shep. I had a feeling you wouldn't answer, but I just wanted to see how you are. I saw the newspapers this morning. Sorry, mate. I don't know what else to say. I saw the video too. You were right – I'm not in it. My fifteen minutes will just have to wait. Which is cold comfort for you, I realise. Anyway, if you need to talk, you know where I am. All right. Later, blood.

I end the call, wondering if he'll get the Warhol reference.

On my laptop, which is warming my thighs, I go to a news website. I select 'UK' and scan the list of stories. Christ, it's everywhere: EX-BOY BAND STAR IN VIDEO SEX SCANDAL. I click on the headline and up pops the story. There are words, maps, photos, timelines.

Perhaps Marlon's e-mailed me? I leave the website and go to Hotmail. I scan my messages, but there's only spam *(Get it up again, I'm a Changed Man, Impotence Treatment, Sweeter tasting sperm Maryellen)*. I wonder if he's left the area. In fact,

I wonder if he's left the country.

Which reminds me – I haven't heard from Lucy P either. I've left messages on her mobile, but she hasn't responded. I still don't know what's happened to her since her arrest on Friday. I compose an e-mail:

> From: shep69@hotmail.com
> To: lucy_p@rocketmail.com
> Subject: ???
>
> Darling Lucy P,
>
> Where are you? I saw you go past the tennis club in a police car on Friday night and assumed you'd been arrested. Are they going to charge you? What's going on? Why haven't you returned my calls?
>
> Get in touch – I'm worried.
>
> The Shep xxx

I log off Hotmail with a heart-jab of loneliness. I go immediately to my favourite contact site. What's happened to Tariq, Marlon and Lucy P should have dampened my appetite. But it hasn't – it's sharpened it. With a lustful eye, I scan the postings. There are plenty of new ones since I checked last week:

> **Tip: keep Britain tidy!!**
> check out the birdlip view park but use your head? Been getting a bad rep because people leaving condoms all over the place!so think else it will be closed before we know it!
> **Posted by: sallysutra**
>
> **Tip: First Time**
> First viewing tonight. Seen a couple in a Mondeo at Loch Leven car park. watched them closely from my car. They didnt mind. I think they were quite new to it as well. Car park is used by gays and pot heads, but not many
> **Posted by: FERRET55**
>
> **Question: Mature couple**
> We're a mature couple, highly experienced, who are interested

> in meeting broadminded couples of any age/persuasion in the Midlands area. Thanking you in advance.
> **Posted by: senior swingers**
>
> **Answer: our experience**
> we've been three times now, each time better than previous, last time we ended up on picnic table with 8–10 guys who each got their cocks sucked by my gf, by the time we'd done around 9 guys had cum over her tits, and she loved it. cant wait till next time, she says she wants to go further and maybe fuck some guys while suckin me/others
> **Posted by: Night Rider**

Then I come to a posting that makes me freeze:

> **Question: Calling cute guy at old tennis club!**
> was at the old tennis club in ——shire with my bf friday night watching hot middle age couple in Volvo and saw v cute guy there wearing dark suit, talking to tall blonde (gf?) but then Old bill showed up and evrybody scattered! Me and my bf are novises, but would luv to meet up with you alone or with gf so get in touch!
> **Posted by: AnyoneForTennis?**

I have to respond quickly; openings for lone men are rare. There are lots of punters out there who'll pretend to be me. I have to pretend to be me before they do:

> **Answer: Re: Calling cute guy at old tennis club!**
> Hi there. Whatever anyone else tells you, I'm the man in the dark suit whom you saw at the old tennis club on Friday night. The blonde woman was not my girlfriend, although she is someone I meet regularly on the circuit. I'd be happy to meet up with you alone, or with her too if she's available. If you want to confirm my identity, give me a call and we can talk (07977 218 638). Alternatively, I could e-mail you a photo and we could take it from there. I look forward to hearing from you.
> **Posted by: The Shep**

I click on 'Send' – my answer slides into the ether. Not a bad night's work.

I return to my Hotmail account, even though I only checked it five minutes ago: no new messages.

I disconnect from the internet. Where the hell *is* everybody?

10

I STAND ON THE DOORSTEP of my parents' house. I breathe in the night air: wet grass, rained on an hour ago; the delicate perfume of a magnolia tree; the metallic whiff of carbon monoxide; and the smell of the night itself. Darkness has a smell of its own.

I walk along the garden path, open the gate – it squeaks briefly – and close it behind me. Instinctively, I look up at my parents' windows. I know they'll be unlit: they've gone out to dinner at a friend's house. They won't be back until later. In fact, if they both decide to drink, they won't be back at all.

Like a fox, I drift through the darkened suburbs. I reach for my iPod and choose some music. I go for *Mezzanine* (1998) by Massive Attack. I hear the slow, distant rumble of 'Angel' – that frightening, brooding build-up. It reminds me of my former life in London; I used to play it in my BMW on my way to work. I look up at the cherry tree as I pass underneath it. Its branches have shed their blossoms; its green leaves are tinted orange by street light.

I'm on my way to meet the couple who spotted me that night at the tennis club. Their online name is AnyoneForTennis?, but their real-life names – or real-life pseudonyms – are Liam and Beccy. We've exchanged a few e-mails; I sent them a digital photo of myself; I even spoke to them on my mobile. I tried to contact Lucy P to invite her along too, but she hasn't answered my texts. I'm rather worried about her. No word from Marlon either. Or Tariq, for that matter.

I'm meeting the couple in the supermarket car park. It was my idea, but they seemed happy to go along with it. It's the perfect place to meet new people: it's close, it's familiar and it's safe. After my last experience there, with the geriatric swingers, I was wary of the new couple's ages. But it turns out that they're younger than I am – both in their late twenties.

I enter the car park, pause and look around. It's deserted, including the blind spot where I told them to park (according to their text message, they're coming in a navy Polo). I check the time: I'm five minutes early. I know I'm being watched and have to keep moving as casually as possible. I continue across the tarmac, kitbag over my shoulder, under the semi-human gaze of the surveillance cameras.

I reach the kennel and relax slightly. I turn round and face the car park: it's only then that I notice a car parked in the far-right corner, headlights off. I can see that it's a Mini, but can't make out its occupants. A lorry rumbles over the road outside, its headlights strobed through the foliage; they flicker, briefly, over the car's grey paintwork.

I hear what sounds like a twig crack behind me; I swivel round. There's nothing there. The sound must have been farther away than I thought. My eyes are drawn to moving shadows under a nearby tree. As my vision adjusts, some outlines take shape. I see two men there, one leaning with his back against the trunk, the other on his knees, working his head in front of the other man's groin. The standing man spots me and thumps his partner on the shoulder; he turns round too, still crouching. I sense that they're about to scarper. Wanting to reassure them, I hold up my palm and call through the night:

'Evening!'

For a moment, they do and say nothing – merely stay as they are, as still as pillars of salt. But when they realise I'm not about to move, they seem to relax. The crouching man holds up his palm too:

'Evening!'

I nod at them both, smiling. 'Don't mind me, I'm just' – I gesture behind me with my thumb, as if I'm hitching a lift – 'you know ... waiting for someone.'

They nod back. We all fall silent.

'Oh, of course, I'll just' – I make a little pirouetting motion in the air with my finger – 'you know ...' Hands in my jacket pockets, I turn round to face the car park. From what I can hear, the action resumes behind me.

After standing in the kennel for three or four minutes, ignoring the rustling and the occasional groan, I see a dark-coloured car enter the car park. I can't tell if it's a Polo, but it's certainly a hatchback. My eyes follow it through the dimness. But instead of driving straight towards me, it follows the complex system of painted arrows on the tarmac, as though the car park is packed rather than near-empty. I interpret this as a sign of nerves: a heightened desire to cling to protocol in the face of uncertainty.

As the car approaches, I step back into the shadow of the tall hedge behind me. I do this for two reasons. First, to make physical room for the car. Second, to put the young couple at their ease. I don't want to stand there, waiting for them, hands in my pockets, like a lonely uncle.

But rather than driving towards the hedge to park with its windscreen facing me, as would be logical, the car does an immaculate three-point turn and parks so that I'm confronted with its rear window. I see from its badge that it's a Corsa, not a Polo; I see from the moonlight that it's black, not navy. Did we get our wires crossed? Did they have to change car at the last minute? This sometimes happens.

My face among the leaves is lit by its reversing lights. The white lights die, then the red lights, then the engine. The car just sits there, about ten metres away, its engine cracking as it cools. I see two figures in the front seats, neither of them moving.

Behind me, through the hedge, I hear a gasp, a muffled cry, then the sound of shuffling.

I wait for a sign from the Corsa: an interior light, a wound-down window, even a beep of the horn. But there's nothing.

Then, one of the windows is lowered. It sounds electric – a surprise in such a modest car. It's the passenger window. I step out from the shadows.

As I walk, I peer through the rear window, trying to get a glimpse of its occupants. But the interior light is off and their heads are obscured by headrests. I approach the passenger window, hands in my jacket pockets. For reasons I can't explain, my fists are clenched. I bend down to the open window: the figures inside are wearing hooded tops, staring straight ahead of them.

'Hello?' I ask, my voice weak and tentative.

The hooded tops turn to me. I see two faces, orange in the street light: thin, young, male.

'Hello,' says one. 'You fucking pervert.'

Just as I'm about to run, I feel a heavy blow across my shoulders. My brain is jarred with confusion. I have the weird sensation that there's a tree behind me and I've just straightened up into one of its branches. Did it spring from the tarmac, like something out of Ovid? Pain, burning, spurts through my shoulder blades.

Then, I feel a second blow: a heavy object slams into my right arm. I hear a crack, feel something move inside the flesh. Pain flashes down my right side, crushes my stomach like a human fist around a plastic cup. I vomit on to the tarmac – then go deaf.

I stagger, my shoes slipping in the liquid. In silence, I see two young men in front of me. Both have shaven heads and are wearing tracksuits. One of them is holding a thick metal pipe, the other is swinging a cricket bat. My deafness breaks up. I hear car doors open, a bottle smash. The man with the cricket bat comes towards me – nimble, light-footed, like a fencer. I want to run, but I'm surrounded by bodies. Swaying, I try to raise my fists to defend myself. But only my left arm moves – my right, dead, just swings from my shoulder. The man with the cricket bat laughs, his jaw lopsided. I'm shoved from behind and stumble forward. There are yells of encouragement. I hear the man grunt, see his mouth twist, watch the cricket bat swing. I smell a puff of alcohol, feel the wood connect.

I feel no pain this time, only numbness. It's the sound that stays with me in the moments afterwards: a deafening *clunk*, as if I've just been hit with an anvil. My ears are roaring with tinnitus. I reel backwards. Warm liquid runs into my left eye, blinding it. Again, I empty my stomach. I stumble across the tarmac, blinking, and hit a wall; it smacks into my body, solid. Where did that come from?

Then I realise that I'm no longer upright, but supine, and that the wall is the ground. I feel gravel against my cheek; in my mouth, I taste blood and gastric acid. I want to scream out for my mother, but can't form the words. All I manage is a husky 'Mu— !' I hear voices, a car ignition, a dog barking in the distance. My right eye, level with the ground, sees a pristine white trainer. I spot a brand name on the leather with a Union Jack beside it.

Then, a fourth blow: an angular object cracks into my ribs. A star of pain explodes in my abdomen. The pain fills my bones, my muscles, my blood.

My mind flickers off, like a light bulb.

11

THE SOUND I HEARD a moment ago triggers a memory in my brain. I'm standing as a boy with my father at the bottom of our back garden. We're watching a bonfire gently smouldering. There's plenty of smoke, but the flames aren't taking. My father, bare-chested, picks up a dry branch from the ground. He twists off its green leaves and fritters them behind him. Mutely, I look up at him; everything he does is awesome, fascinating, heroic. He snaps the branch over his knee – I flinch at the sharp *crack!* – and throws it onto the pile. An orange tongue of fire licks around the branch. We watch this flame in silence.

12

THE LIGHT BULB FLICKERS ON. The car park is deserted. A violet street light is blinking overhead. My body is a sack of wheat: a dead weight. The pain distends my body from my toes to my face. It comes in nauseous waves. My mouth is dry and sticky. The tarmac bites my cheek.

13

I HEAR A SOUND IN THE NIGHT, feel a wetness on my neck. Startled, I try to lift my head. But it's pinned to the ground as if somebody's pressing their foot on it. The pain of exertion makes me cry out. I hear a scampering noise fading away from me. My right eye blinks open: a fox is running across the car park.

14

THE SOUND OF GROANING. Limbs writhing over the tarmac. I retch with pain, but on an empty stomach. Human voices getting closer. Footsteps coming towards me. I tense with terror. The beeping of mobile-phone buttons. Fingertips stroking my face. Light touching my eyelids. Weightless.

part five

nonunhappiness

1

I OPEN MY EYES. No, not quite: my eyes open. I blink to clear them, but they remain smeary. The predominant colour is white. Spokes of light are cartwheeling through the window.

At first, I assume I'm in my bedroom. But my bedroom is dark and cosy. It's only after a moment that I realise where I am. It's not so much what I see, as what I smell: disinfectant, plastic, soap, linen.

My senses are coming back to life. Reawakening.

2

MY VISION IS CLEARING. I tip my head forward to look down at my own body. I'm lying in bed with my chest and arms uncovered. I appear to be wearing a tissue-paper toga. My right arm is in plaster; my left wrist is bandaged. I can't see the rest of me.

I wiggle my fingers, then my toes. I shift my head from side to side. Apart from a stiffness in my neck, my plastered arm and my bandaged wrist, everything seems to be normal. At least, I can feel and move everything.

Images from the car park drift back to me: the hooded faces, the man with the cricket bat, the fox crossing the tarmac.

But they don't scare me. They feel like images from a half-forgotten dream – floating away from me, harmless. Polaroids on the sea's surface.

I float away, too, on a swell of indifference. Nothing can touch me.

3

I LOOK AROUND MY BED. There are machines on one side and a table on the other. On the table is a bowl of fruit, some flowers and a card. I pick up the card with my right hand. It shows golden retrievers, tongues hanging out, staring into the middle distance heroically. Inside is a handwritten message:

Dear Shep,

We thought you might end up here, so we just wanted to say GET WELL SOON. We feel terrible – if we'd arrived on time, maybe it wouldn't have happened.

Please get in touch if there's anything we can do.

Best wishes,
Liam & Beccy

Liam and Beccy? I don't know anyone called Liam and Beccy. I wonder if I have amnesia. The prospect doesn't frighten me.

I hear voices in the corridor. They have a shimmering quality, as if refracted through water. Not all my senses are back to normal yet. I hide the card under my duvet. Turning my head towards the door, I recognise my surroundings. I'm in the same room as Tariq when he was admitted here: I recognise the faceless decor, the dreary aerial vista.

The Middle Eastern doctor comes in. She's wearing a white coat and has tied her hair in a firm chignon. Even through my drowsiness, I find her ravishing. I imagine pulling her towards me for a kiss using the stethoscope around her neck – the way strippers do with feathery scarves in films.

She's followed closely by my parents, who shuffle in worriedly. My mother is holding a British Museum carrier bag. They look like an elderly couple who've had a nice day out in London. As soon as my mother sees me, she crumples into tears. My father hovers in the background, navy-blue-blazered, hands behind his back.

I smile reassuringly. It's only then, as my face changes shape, that I realise I have tubes coming out of my nostrils.

'Oh, Jeremy!' says my mother, putting down the carrier bag and clasping my right hand.

'Hello,' I reply.

The three of them discuss what happened to me. They do this as if I'm in another room – or catatonic – rather than lying in bed in front of them, blinking. It turns out that I have an impressive gamut of injuries: a right arm broken in two places, a fractured wrist (the left, thank Christ), a four-inch gash in my scalp, a cracked rib, concussion and extensive bruising on my back and sides. But I've escaped spinal injuries or brain damage, which is a bonus.

'They went easy on me,' I joke.

The three of them look at me. Nobody laughs.

'But what were you *doing* in that car park in the middle of the night?' asks my mother, nervously, still holding my hand.

I'm about to say I was walking the dog, when I remember we don't have one. Could I say I was walking the cat? No. Samuel, the bastard, would never back me up.

'I'd been out with some people from work,' I lie, 'and I took a short cut past the supermarket.'

My mother doesn't look convinced.

'I think the police would like to speak to you,' says the doctor, gravely, her arms folded over the clipboard.

'Fine,' I say.

But I have no intention of speaking to the police; or, if I do, I'll be as unhelpful as possible. Given my lifestyle, the less contact I have with Plod the better. God knows how much surveillance footage I've appeared in over the years. And what could I tell them anyway? That I had the shit kicked out of me by a bunch of violent yobs? My town is full of them. England is full of them. I couldn't identify them if they were lying in bed next to me.

'Are you in pain?' asks my father.

'No,' I reply, shaking my head. 'In fact, I feel better than ever. I wonder if the attack did me good in some way. Whether it ... *purified* me.'

'It's the morphine,' says the doctor, coolly. 'It's affecting your mood. It's making you feel euphoric.'

'Oh.'

Everyone nods, as if to say: *that explains it, then.*

I suddenly understand why people do heroin. In fact, I'm thinking of doing some myself when I get out of here. I make a mental note to go back to the railway station to hang out with those junkies. Maybe they could give me a few pointers?

'So how's Samuel?'

I ask this not because I care, but because I want to deflect attention from the circumstances of my attack – and the one topic guaranteed to get my parents talking is the cat. Once I've lit the tabby touchpaper, there'll be no stopping them. And off they go again. The doctor stands there with an expression that says: they're all mad.

After ten minutes of talking about Samuel – his allergies, his sleep patterns, his bowel movements – my parents pipe down. By this time, the visiting period is almost over. Perfect.

My father sighs, looking at his watch. 'Well, I suppose we ought to be going.'

'What are your plans for tonight?'

'We're off to play bridge at Rod and Julie's.'

'Oh, lovely.'

'But we'll come and visit you tomorrow,' adds my mother, squeezing my hand. 'We *promise*.'

I shrug. 'Only if you want to. You needn't worry.' My eyes meet the doctor's – dark, feline, liquid. 'I'm in very capable hands.' She doesn't respond to my look in the slightest.

'Oh, and I brought you some things,' says my mother, putting the carrier bag next to my bed. 'In case you get bored.'

After they've left, I look inside the carrier bag. My mother is a genius: she's brought me my notebooks, my laptop, my mobile phone (although now they know I have one, I'll have to pretend to lose it), the novel I was reading (*L'Extension de la Domaine de la Lutte* by Michel Houellebecq) and a broadsheet newspaper. In fact, all I need now are condoms, KY jelly and a good-sized banana, and I'd be right back in business.

The first thing I do is check my phone for messages. To my delight, there's a text from Lucy P. My heart purrs as I open it:

> hi Shep, thanx 4 your email. just to say im fine after the night @ the tennis club. I got arested but let off with a warning (v cute officer!) sorry I havent been in touch but I wanted to lay low. how r u? Lets meet up soon!

Clearly, she doesn't know what's happened to me. I check my voice messages. There's only one, from Marlon:

> Shep, it's me. I found out what happened after I phoned you at work. Sounds bad. You poor, poor bastard. I hope you're all right. Thanks for your message, by the way. Mate, it's all gone tits up. Stacy's moved out, my family's not speaking to me and I've got fuck all work. But get this – I keep getting calls from publishers in London, asking me to write a memoir. You know, about the scene an' that. They'd pay me up front, so I'm seriously thinking about it. But how do I write a book? Maybe you could help me when you're all patched up? Have a think about it. Anyway, give me a bell when you're up to it. Later, blood.

I put my phone back in the carrier bag, where my laptop lies in its zip-up case. I should boot it up to check my e-mail, but I don't know if I can get online here.

I'm distracted by a nurse passing my bed. I watch her cross the room in front of me. I recognise her from reception when I came to visit Tariq. I decide to try my luck – with the one word I know in Polish:

'*Cześć!*'

'*Cześć!*' she replies, with a startled laugh.

Bingo. I check her ring finger: a gold wedding band glints on it. Still, when did that ever stop anybody? Monogamy is dead – if it ever lived in the first place.

After she's left, and feeling at a loose end, I take out the newspaper. Sitting up in bed, I flick through it (delicately, with my right hand). I stop at a story in the 'Home news' section:

Refugee, 14, raped at knifepoint

A female refugee was raped at knifepoint last night in W—— in ——shire.

The girl, who is fourteen years old and from Iran, where she and her family were persecuted for being practising Christians, was attacked in a supermarket car park on her way home from the town centre. She cannot be named for legal reasons.

——shire police believe the attack may be a vigilante response to the rape of a local schoolgirl by a Somalian asylum seeker last month.

A man is being held in custody. Police describe him as white and local to the area.

I put down the newspaper and close my eyes. I feel so tired, suddenly.

4

WHEN I OPEN MY EYES, Tariq is standing right in front of me.

At least, I think he is. I can't be certain; I'm too woozy. I frown at his handsome face. He blinks at me, patiently. He says something to me, but I can't understand him. I try to ask him to repeat it, but the words won't come; I feel as if I'm speaking with a mouthful of toffee. He says something else, but I can't fathom it.

I blink – and he's vanished.

5

THE ONLY SIGN THAT TIME is passing is the changing light through the window – from oily black to metallic blue to watery yellow. The smell of fruit unearths a childhood memory: the apple tree, in blossom, at the bottom of our garden.

I reach over to my bedside table for a glass of water. I see a white envelope leaning against it. On the front is a single word: 'Shep'. Strange that it doesn't say 'Jeremy'. There's no stamp or address, so it must have been hand-delivered. I tear it open. The card inside has two kittens on the front, peeking out of a ribboned straw basket. I suspect it was bought from the hospital gift shop. I read the message, written in shaky red Biro:

Shep,

I herd you were here from Tony. I wanted to visit you because you visit me. I am hoping you feel better now. I have put some grapes in your bowl of fruits.

The sene is dificult now because we have no places – the picnic point is visited by many jurnalists. Police are in the tennis club and the supermarket. Every body is very frustrated with this!

But I hope we can find a new place soon. Please send us an e-mail when you are out and we can enjoy again.

Your friend,

Tariq

So – he's back. And not a moment too soon. That's all the encouragement I need. I take my laptop from the carrier bag and unfold it on my bed. With the help of my glamorous assistant, Magda the Polish nurse, I connect it to the internet. I log on to my Hotmail account. Sitting up in bed, I write an e-mail to Tariq, Marlon and Lucy P:

From: shep69@hotmail.com
To: marlonman@yahoo.co.uk, lucy_p@rocketmail.com, tariq@———gov.uk

Subject: Sunday night

Dear all,

It's The Shep here, writing live from my hospital bed. Thanks for your messages and words of support. I'm still very delicate, but getting better by the day.

I miss the scene, however. I know a lot of our favourite sites have been exposed recently, but I've thought of an alternative – the car park at the back of this hospital. It's often empty, from what I've seen, and it's well concealed by trees. We can't be sure that it's safe, of course, but there's only one way to find out.

So let's give it a try. I suggest we meet there at eleven o'clock on Sunday night. I hope you can all make it.

The Shep xxx

PS Could you bring some condoms and lube? I'm not sure I can buy any in the hospital gift shop.

PPS Strictly no cameras – analogue, digital, video or otherwise!

6

AS THE WEEK GOES BY, I make astonishing physical progress. The human body is a miracle of self-repair. By Friday, I've been moved out of intensive care into a general ward. I'm now well enough to walk around the hospital, unaided. I'm hardly at my best – my right arm is in a sling, my left wrist is bandaged, I'm assailed by stabbing pains and I limp like Quasimodo – but at least I'm mobile. The truth is, I like my life here; it's a model of asceticism. I can read, write and think as much as I like. There's nothing to buy, nothing to sell, nothing to use up. I wonder if I could engineer a long-term stay, Yossarian-style? Perhaps I could pretend to be more decrepit than I really am? Maybe I could feign a serious mental illness? Something tells me I could do either without much difficulty.

But it's not all roses. There are two thorns in my side here. First, I'm no longer tripping on morphine. Second, my penis badly needs a workout.

Still, I don't have long to wait. Now that it's Sunday night, I'm virtually twitching with excitement. I'm sitting up in bed with a hard-on of pure anticipation. I check my watch: 10.49 p.m. Time to get a move on.

The small ward is full of old people, dozing and snoring. The only exception is a man about my age, lying in the bed opposite. He looks as if he's asleep. The top of his head is bandaged up. I've no idea what his name is. We haven't exchanged a word.

As I leave my bed, the bedsprings creak (the harder you try to be quiet, the more noise you make). The man stirs in his bed opposite. I switch off my bedside lamp, take two pillows from my bed, and stuff them under the sheets to make them look like a sleeping body.

But they're not very convincing. I need a papier-mâché head, like the one Clint Eastwood uses in *Escape From Alcatraz* (1979). But I don't think ten minutes will be long enough to make one.

Then I have a brainwave: honesty. Or mock-honesty. I remove the pillows and put them back in place. I take a white envelope from my bedside table – the envelope Tariq's card came in – and scribble a message on it:

> *Hello!*
>
> *I've just popped to the toilet. I think the one on this floor is occupied, so I might try a different floor. I'm a bit constipated though, so it could take a while. Don't worry!*

I prop the envelope on my pillow, put on my tartan dressing gown and step into my Harry Potter slippers (a gift from my mother last Christmas). I creep along the corridor towards the lift. At the end of the corridor are light, noise and activity. A nurse comes out of a nearby ward, so I dart behind a coffee machine. The sudden movement slides a skewer through my ribs; I wince from the pain of it. The nurse shuffles past, oblivious, studying her clipboard.

I leave my hiding place and limp towards the lift. I press the button and wait, restless. When it finally arrives, the lift *pings!* more loudly than any lift I've ever heard in my life. Its metal doors rumble open; I hobble inside.

As I whirr and tremble downwards, I check the buttons on my pyjama bottoms: I don't want my boner popping out. I feel excited, but reflective. I lean against the side of the lift, staring at the tumbling numbers. It wasn't long ago that I was travelling upwards in this same lift, on my way to visit Tariq, my ageing body unharmed.

7

I STOP ON THE GROUND FLOOR and *ping!* out in Casualty. Even on a Sunday night, the place is rammed. Casualty is my favourite part of any hospital – because it's the most surreal. The world over, people sit in their moulded plastic chairs in exactly the same outfits they were in when they had their accidents. As I shuffle towards the exit, I have a look around. I spot, at random, a woman in paint-flecked dungarees, head tipped back, pinching her bloody nose; a young man in a Chelsea strip pressing a pork chop to his knee; a red-eyed girl in a McDonald's uniform nursing her bandaged hand; and an old man in paisley pyjamas, yawning, apparently unharmed. If Heaven has a waiting room, Casualty is what it will look like. Bloodier, perhaps.

The glass doors part noiselessly. For a moment, I stand outside – eyes closed, hair wind-blown. It feels good to be in the world again. When I open my eyes, I see a sign for the second car park. It's set back from the road, partially obscured by branches. I follow its fluorescent arrow, limping along the pavement.

The pavement leads to the back of the hospital. With every step, my pain is getting worse. But I ignore it. I feel horny, driven, gripped. As the pavement curves round, the car park opens in front of me. It's hemmed in by Scots pines and is weakly lit. In other words, it's perfect. It's also deserted;

deserted, that is, except for a sky-blue Jaguar and a battered Honda Civic.

As I set off through the amber mist, my mind begins to wander. One often takes stock of one's life, I've found, at unexpected moments – carrying shopping bags home through the drizzle; pausing during the gardening to stare into a flower bed; leaning back in one's chair at work, twisting a paperclip. Crossing the car park with my arm in a sling, I can't help wondering how it came to this: to be a patient in a provincial English hospital, limping towards a Honda Civic to engage in group sex with an Arab refugee, a disgraced ex-pop star and a grey-eyed nymphomaniac.

All in all, however, on this humid night in June, my prevailing emotion is one of gratitude. How could it be otherwise? I have everything I need to lead a contented, if not happy, existence. Happiness, in adulthood, is a tall order; contentment, I think, is far more realistic. Or what e. e. cummings called *nonunhappiness*.

But my nonunhappiness springs less from what I do than what I don't do: in a Hippocratic spirit, I do no harm. I may not exactly relieve suffering, but nor do I inflict any. The facts of my life are these: I'm vegetarian, childless, I don't own a car, I try not to fly, I buy only what I need, I recycle my glass and paper. True, I don't liberate animals from research laboratories, or climb trees to defy logging companies, or lobby governments over African debt. But by the low moral standards of the society into which I was born, my life is an ethical one. At least, it's about as ethical as it can be given the webs of exploitation from which Western lifestyles are spun. My hands may not be clean, but they're cleaner than most.

Which is more than I can say for my mind: my mind, I'm relieved to say, is as filthy as ever. But that doesn't lead to any suffering either. The sex in which I participate, however distasteful it may be to some – to you – is strictly mutually consenting. I wouldn't have it any other way.

And I could hardly wish for a more consenting group of people. I stop in front of the Honda, about ten metres away. Tariq is leaning against the driver's door, his right bicep still bandaged. Marlon is standing beside the car, wearing a big dirty grin. Lucy P is reclined on the bonnet, her skirt riding up her thighs. It's quite a welcome.

'Evening,' I say, with a slow nod to the threesome.

'What kept you?' asks Marlon, smiling. 'You're thirty seconds late.'

I lift my left leg: the one that's making me limp. 'Not as limber as I used to be.'

'So how are you?' asks Tariq, arms folded.

'Not bad,' I say, 'in the circumstances. No permanent injuries, contrary to appearances. I could live without the pain, though. How are you?'

He shrugs. 'Better than before. I still take pills each day. But everything is okay, more or less.'

I point to his arm. 'What about your tattoo?'

'Gone,' he replies. 'But when my skin is normal, I will get a new one.'

'Good for you,' I say.

Lucy P crosses her legs and looks me up and down. 'So, Shep – are you sure you're up to this?'

I tip my head to one side sardonically. '*Please*. I'm not that bad. Are *you*, more like? After your brush with the law, how do we know you're not under police surveillance?'

'Well let's just say I've been seeing a bit of that handsome officer,' she says, 'and I'm confident he won't talk.'

I shake my head. 'Jesus.'

She blinks at me, sexily.

'And what about you, Tolstoy?' I turn to Marlon. 'Have you started your memoir yet?'

He laughs. 'Waiting for you to help me, blood.'

'What other news? Have you seen Stacy?'

His face turns more serious. 'No. She's gone – and she's

taken the kids with her. I don't know where she is. I think she might be at her mum's place.' His expression lightens; he lifts his arms either side of him. 'But who needs a family when I have this?'

'My thoughts entirely,' says Lucy P.

'So what now?' I ask, looking around at them. 'Shall we get started?'

'Not yet,' says Tariq, shaking his head. 'We wait for two others.'

'Really?' I frown. 'Who?'

'A couple I met on the web,' says Marlon. 'We don't know much about them. Drive a small car – some kind of hatchback.'

'And when are they arriving?' I ask.

Lucy P nods over my shoulder. 'Now, by the looks of it.'

I turn to see a car enter the car park. I recognise the model and I recognise the colour. My heart contracts, my bowels turn to water. For a moment, I'm paralysed.

Then I run – for the nearby trees and the darkness they promise. I hear the others scattering behind me: car doors slam, engines tear the silence. For the first time in days, I feel no pain, only numbness.

epilogue

SINCE OUR FIRST CONVERSATION in the hospital that night, and after studying his multifarious writings – which gave me intimate access not only to his lifestyle, but also to his deepest feelings and thoughts – Jeremy Shepherd had been much on my mind. Like a biographer who vicariously lives the life of his subject, dead or alive, I developed a strong affinity with the author of *The Isle of Dogs*. During the editing process, I often wondered where he might be, not to mention what he might be doing, while I was riding the Tube or reading his diary by lamplight.

I did attempt to stay in touch with him. As soon as I received proofs from the printer (minus my prologue and epilogue), and despite his flagrant lack of interest in this book, I sent him a copy for correction. On a compliments slip, I wrote a brief message:

Dear Jeremy,

I hope you're well. I wondered whether you'd like to make any last-minute changes? If not, it will go to press as it is.

It would always be a pleasure to hear from you.

Best wishes,
Daniel Davies

Needless to say, I didn't hear back. Then, about a fortnight later, I arrived at work to find a brown paper parcel on my desk. When I inspected it, I realised it was the proof copy I'd sent out. On the front, Jeremy Shepherd's address had been crossed through with a single line. Above it, written in purple ink, were the words: 'PLEASE RETURN TO SENDER'.

The following Saturday, I drove home to see my parents – a visit I'd had planned for some weeks. I'd tried to organise a meeting with Jeremy Shepherd beforehand: I wanted to take him out for dinner so we could catch up, and – I secretly hoped – discuss the possibility of future projects. But, as elusive as ever, he ignored my calls and e-mails. I even thought about driving to some of his favourite sites on the circuit in the hope of running into him.

At the tail end of my journey, I stopped at a service station on the outskirts of town. At the counter, I bought a local newspaper, the *F—— Argus*, as has been my ritual for some time. Later that evening, while my parents were nodding off in front of *Newsnight*, I read the paper with the cat on my lap. On page 5, I found this:

'Sociable' civil servant dies from overdose

A civil servant from F—— has died at home after taking a lethal overdose of painkillers.

Jeremy Michael Shepherd, 39, had been prescribed medication for chronic pain following his discharge from S—— Hospital in T——. He had received treatment for serious injuries after an unprovoked attack in June left him unconscious in a car park.

Those close to Mr Shepherd say he had become severely depressed and reclusive in the weeks since leaving hospital.

'We never saw him any more,' said friend Lucinda P——. 'He used to be very sociable, sending constant texts and e-mails. But then it all

> went quiet. He just stopped coming out. I suspect he had his reasons.'
>
> After a successful career as an editor and journalist, Mr Shepherd worked at the Ministry of — for five years. He lived at home with his parents, Henry and Rosemary Shepherd. He was unmarried.
>
> A funeral service will be held on Monday.

I was stunned. The next day, first thing, I found his parents' number in the telephone directory. I spoke to his father, who sounded blank and devastated: 'We just keep asking *why*,' he said, 'though I know he was in terrible pain.' I told him I was a friend of Jeremy's from London – the man who'd sent the parcel he'd returned. Would he and his wife mind if I came to the funeral? Not in the slightest, he said. In fact, they'd welcome my presence: 'Attendance is looking rather sparse, I'm afraid.'

The next day, after phoning my office to relay the bad news, I attended the funeral of Jeremy Michael Shepherd. It took place at a small church near the house in which he'd spent his childhood – and to which he'd returned as an adult. I knew this church and cemetery well: I'd passed them many times, usually on my bike – a silver Raleigh Grifter – while I too was growing up in the town.

It was an unremarkable day, blustery and tepid. The wind tugged my anorak with the sound of sail. There were six of us around the grave, plus the vicar. The dark-wood coffin was lowered into the earth.

Mr and Mrs Shepherd stood together, hand in hand. I realised that Jeremy Shepherd had looked more like his mother. From their descriptions in *The Isle of Dogs*, I recognised the other mourners. There was Tariq, a startlingly handsome man. There was Lucy P, looking lithe and athletic. And there was Marlon, wearing wraparound shades and a black baseball cap. They were discreet, silent and respectful. Lucy P wept a little; Marlon put his arm around her.

As we drifted away from the grave, Tariq and Marlon walked with Jeremy's parents. Lucy P walked a little way behind them. This was my chance. In another minute, we'd all arrive at the car park, where the group would re-form. If I was going to ask her, I had to do it now.

I approached her and introduced myself as 'a close friend of The Shep's'. She was courteous, but guarded. For a few moments, we walked in silence.

'So what happened?' I asked.

It was blunt, I realised, but I had little choice: I had about thirty seconds.

'What d'you mean, what happened?'

She sounded confused, rather than indignant, which emboldened me: 'That night, at the hospital, in the car park. When The Shep came out to meet you. Why did he run like that?'

She turned to look at me: her eyes were pale grey, just as Jeremy had described them. 'He panicked,' she said, returning her gaze to the ground. 'And so did we.'

'But why?' I asked. 'Who were they? Which car showed up?'

She didn't answer.

'Was it a grey Mini?'

Silence.

'A black Corsa?'

'Look,' she said, without making eye contact. 'Do you have an e-mail address or something? Some way I can contact you?'

'Of course.'

I took a business card from my wallet and handed it to her. She slipped it into her pocket as we reached the car park, where the others were waiting for us.

For over a week, I heard nothing. Then, one afternoon, while I was working at my desk on a spreadsheet, an e-mail arrived. It contained two words:

yellow Peugeot